KT-521-923

 STOCKPO ᵃries

Stockport Libraries

C2000003125392

Born and raised just outside Toronto, Ontario, **Amy Ruttan** fled the big city to settle down with the country boy of her dreams. After the birth of her second child Amy was lucky enough to realise her lifelong dream of becoming a romance author. When she's not furiously typing away at her computer she's mum to three wonderful children who use her as a personal taxi and chef.

Also by Amy Ruttan

Perfect Rivals…
Tempting Nashville's Celebrity Doc
Unwrapped by the Duke
Alejandro's Sexy Secret
His Pregnant Royal Bride
Convenient Marriage, Surprise Twins
Navy Doc on Her Christmas List
The Surgeon King's Secret Baby

Discover more at millsandboon.co.uk.

A MUMMY FOR
HIS DAUGHTER

AMY RUTTAN

Stockport Library
and Information Service

D03125392   CHU

MILLS & BOON

All rights reserved including the right of reproduction in whole or in part in any form. This edition is published by arrangement with Harlequin Books S.A.

This is a work of fiction. Names, characters, places, locations and incidents are purely fictional and bear no relationship to any real life individuals, living or dead, or to any actual places, business establishments, locations, events or incidents. Any resemblance is entirely coincidental.

This book is sold subject to the condition that it shall not, by way of trade or otherwise, be lent, resold, hired out or otherwise circulated without the prior consent of the publisher in any form of binding or cover other than that in which it is published and without a similar condition including this condition being imposed on the subsequent purchaser.

® and TM are trademarks owned and used by the trademark owner and/or its licensee. Trademarks marked with ® are registered with the United Kingdom Patent Office and/or the Office for Harmonisation in the Internal Market and in other countries.

First published in Great Britain 2018
by Mills & Boon, an imprint of HarperCollins*Publishers*
1 London Bridge Street, London, SE1 9GF

Large Print edition 2018

© 2018 Amy Ruttan

ISBN: 978-0-263-07302-7

MIX
Paper from
responsible sources
FSC™ C007454

This book is produced from independently certified FSC™ paper to ensure responsible forest management. For more information visit www.harpercollins.co.uk/green.

Printed and bound in Great Britain
by CPI Group (UK) Ltd, Croydon, CR0 4YY

This book is dedicated to everyone who has been lost and has found their way home.

CHAPTER ONE

I HATE FLYING. I hate flying.

Evelyn closed her eyes and gripped the arm-rests tighter as the Cessna C207 Skycraft she was flying in was jostled by turbulence. And being in a small plane that only seated seven people meant that the turbulence *really* rattled her around, making her stomach twist and knot in apprehension.

Although it wasn't just the turbulence that was doing that to her.

She'd thought in the twenty years since she'd been here that her hometown might have built a road from Sitka to Wolf's Harbor, but no.

Nothing seemed to have changed. Wolf's Harbor was still relying on the service of bush pilots and a small airport and harbor to service the larger hub of Sitka. Although there was a ferry service to Juneau, it took three hours to drive to the ferry terminal and another four hours to cross the channel. That was if the ferry was running. The fastest way was still by air.

Evelyn would have preferred a boat excursion from Sitka to Wolf's Harbor, but there were no vessels departing on the eight-hour journey from Sitka through Cross Sound and into the small inlet of Wolf's Harbor. The Cessna had been her only option.

She didn't like airplanes, even though she was used to flying. Her grandmother had loved taking trips all over the world, but even though air travel was second nature to her she didn't like it any better.

The plane rocked again but the other people who were on the same flight didn't pay any attention to it. They were calm and just rocking with the turbulence as if it was nothing. Of course they were probably used to it.

Evelyn was not. She was used to first class. She wasn't used to a bush plane way of life, nor to this level of turbulence where the pilot would probably have to crab land on the Tarmac because of the wind shear.

The first time she'd flown on a Cessna had been when she'd left Wolf's Harbor—or rather when she'd been taken from Wolf's Harbor.

She'd never got to go back.

Of course she'd been only ten when she'd gone to live in Boston. Her father had been killed by a runaway logging truck when he'd gone out one evening. Her mother—who'd died when Evelyn was four—had been Tlingit, and her maternal grandmother and uncle had lived in Wolf's Harbor, but Evelyn hadn't heard from them in twenty years.

When she'd first left she'd written letters to them, but nothing had ever come back. She'd been devastated, but her paternal grandmother had taught her to be tough. To harden her heart against disappointment.

Besides, it was really *her* fault that her father had died. It was no wonder her mother's family had written her off. Her father had been the beloved town doctor for years until that accident. It had been for the best that she'd left.

Still, it had torn a hole in her soul. She'd got world experience, and a great education, but as a child she hadn't wanted to leave Wolf's Harbor.

A social service worker from Juneau had come to take her away. Her father's estranged mother in Boston had got custody of her. And, as a child, she really hadn't had a say....

"I don't want to leave," Evelyn protested, clutching her small rag doll and looking back at her father's log cabin with longing.

She loved her cozy home in the forest, where she'd used to wait for her father to come home. But he was never coming back. Her father was gone—and all because he had been on his way to see that woman. The woman who wanted to replace her mother.

"You have no choice," the social worker said, kneeling in front of her.

She could see the pain in the woman's eyes.

"I'm sorry, Evelyn, but your grandmother in Boston is looking forward to your arrival and she's your legal guardian now. Your father didn't have a will and a judge has ruled in your paternal grandmother's favor. You have to go live with her."

"I don't want to go to Boston."

"I know." The social worker squeezed her shoulder. "I wish you could stay too."

Evelyn picked up her knapsack, which held all her belongings, and took the social worker's hand as they climbed into the taxi cab which drove them to the airport.

The Cessna was waiting and there were other

passengers climbing on board. She gripped the social worker's hand as she looked back at the town.

The taxi cab driver—Uncle Yazzie—had tears in his eyes as he waved goodbye to her.

"Why can't I stay with my uncle? Why can't I stay with my grandmother? They can take care of me. I want to stay with them."

"Your grandmother in Boston has guardianship over you. The court has decided that you have to go to Boston, Evelyn. I'm so sorry. I know that you want to stay, but you have to be a brave girl. It will be okay."

A lump formed in Evelyn's throat. She was leaving everything she knew, everything she loved, to live with a stranger.

Uncle Yazzie scrubbed a hand over his face. "Don't worry. We'll see each other again soon."

Evelyn nodded and tried to fight back the tears as she walked away from the only family she'd known.

She would never forgive herself for not stopping her father from going out that night to see Jocelyn—the woman he'd wanted to marry. If she'd stopped him he'd still be alive...

"Ladies and gents, we're now making our descent into Wolf's Harbor. Please fasten your seat-belt."

The pilot made the same announcement in Tlingit and Evelyn felt sad that she'd almost forgotten her mother's language. She understood it still, but when was the last time she'd spoken it?

Evelyn couldn't remember. Her grandmother had banned all talk of Alaska and anything of her past because it had been too painful for her, and Evelyn hadn't wanted to make her grandmother upset. Her grandmother had blamed Alaska for taking her son away, for her having had to disinherit him. Alaska had ruined her father's promising surgical career.

Evelyn had still loved Alaska, but had said nothing to her grandmother about her love for her former home. She had always been worried her grandmother would send her away, so she'd just tried to please the woman.

She hadn't wanted to be alone. She hadn't wanted to be sent away again.

That trip to Boston... She'd known then what alone felt like. It had been terrible, and she'd never wanted to feel that way again.

Except now you are alone!

And it was her fault again this time.

She'd been with Nathan for two years, but her career had always been more important to her. Nathan had a great surgical practice in Minnesota, and he wanted to settle down and get married. Only that was the last thing that Evelyn wanted.

She didn't want a family. One that could be taken away from her in an instant. One she didn't deserve.

There was a part of her that should have felt sorrow over losing Nathan, but she felt numb and a little bit relieved.

He'd accused her once of being cold. And maybe she was.

Of course being cold meant that you kept your heart intact. Not feeling was her armor. Her protection against pain. Her grandmother had taught her to guard her heart in order to avoid pain. Emotions were for the weak. And it served her well as a surgeon.

She took a deep breath and looked out through the small window to see Wolf's Harbor come into view through the misty summer rain that was clinging to the mountains.

Her heart skipped a beat and her palms were sweaty, but she wasn't sure if that was from the turbulence or from seeing the place where she'd been born. A place she'd never thought she'd see again.

The sight of the boats moored at the town dock and even the vessels that were out on the eerily calm water made her stomach flip in anticipation. It was just as beautiful as she remembered.

For the first year of her life in Boston she'd dreamed about Wolf's Harbor, dreamed about her father, and then what she remembered had begun to fade as she'd integrated into life in Boston.

Her grandmother had been distant and mourning her son's decision to head to Alaska, and her grandmother's grief and bitterness had seeped into their life in Boston. So they'd traveled a lot. Boston had been their home base, but she had always felt her grandmother had traveled so she wouldn't have a moment to grieve for her son. Boston might have been a base, but it had never felt like home.

She'd excelled in school, to please her grandmother, and had gone to Dartmouth and then Harvard Medical School. During her last year at Harvard her grandmother had died, but Evelyn's time there had seemed to please her. The more

Evelyn had excelled, the more her grandmother had seemed happy with her.

She'd done her residency in Seattle, and earned a fellowship in obstetrics and neonatal medicine. She'd been searching for a new challenge when she'd been contacted by a surgeon friend in Sitka, who had begged her to come and take over her practice while she went on a three-month honeymoon.

Evelyn had thought it would be good—she just hadn't had any idea that part of the practice was a rotation in Wolf's Harbor that her friend shared with a couple other OB/GYNs and that she worked there every three months. And the day Evelyn had landed in Sitka had been the day she was to start her three-month rotation in Wolf's Harbor.

At first she'd thought of not going, of letting her friend down, but she longed to see Wolf's Harbor again. To help where she hadn't been able to help before.

She owed it to her father.

To her home.

Not your home.

She had to remind herself of that. There was no place for her here. Not anymore. All she had to do was step in for the next three months and then she could leave with a lighter conscience.

Dr. Pearson, the OB/GYN who was finishing his rotation in Wolf's Harbor, would be waiting for her at the town's clinic, where he'd hand over the keys to the clinic, and the furnished apartment they used during rotation, and would show her around before he drove back to Juneau.

The plane landed with a bump on the small gravel airstrip and the props slowed down as the Cessna taxied to the terminal. When it had come to a stop and shut down, the pilot hopped into gear, opening the door as the ground crew pushed over the stairwell, and Evelyn could feel the hatches being opened to unload the cargo.

The two other occupants—both men—grabbed their duffel bags and headed off the plane.

Evelyn took a deep breath. *You got this.*

She slung her laptop bag over her shoulder and unbuckled. When she stepped out of the Cessna she was hit by the scent of salt water, rain and damp. There was a clanging from the buoys out on the mist-shrouded water. It hadn't changed.

Home.

Evelyn closed her eyes to stop the tears that were threatening.

"Come here, Evie."

Her father held open his arms and she ran to him, pressing her face against the soft flannel jacket he wore.

"I love you, Daddy."

Her dad kissed the top of her head and smiled, his blue-gray eyes twinkling.

"I love you, too, Evie."

"Do you need help, miss?"

Evelyn shook the memory away and glanced down to see the pilot, in a flannel jacket that was similar to the one her father had used to wear, holding out his hand to her.

She straightened her spine and beamed brightly at him, taking his hand as he helped her down onto the Tarmac.

"Do you need help with your luggage?" the pilot asked.

"No, thank you. I'm okay." Evelyn shifted the weight of her carry-on bag on her shoulder as she walked onto the chip-sealed portion of the airstrip. She picked up her suitcase from outside the plane, where it had been unloaded, and popped up the handle to roll it.

A gust of wind tossed her hair in her face and

she cursed herself for not tying it back before she headed for the small terminal.

I wonder if anyone will remember who I am?

A knot formed in her stomach—because it had been twenty years since she had been taken away…twenty years since her father died. She remembered some faces, but she was sure most folks were long gone.

Like her maternal grandmother.

And her classmates at the small village school wouldn't remember her.

It was for the best that they didn't.

It was *her* fault her father had left that night in the rain and died. She should have stopped him.

She'd taken away Wolf's Harbor's finest doctor. Now she was here to make it right.

Or as right as she could in the limited amount of time she was here.

The terminal was quiet. Everyone was dealing with cargo, rather than the few passengers. The other two who had been on her plane were long gone. They had somewhere to go. Loved ones to see.

She had no one.

"Can I help you?"

Evelyn turned to the young woman who was

manning the counter at the Wolf's Harbor terminal.

"I'm looking for directions to the town clinic."

The young woman smiled brightly. "It's about a fifteen-minute walk from here. Do you want me to call you a taxi?"

"That would be great. Thank you," Evelyn said, smiling back.

The young woman nodded, but didn't pick up the phone. Instead she got up off her stool, and Evelyn saw the round belly of a pregnant woman under her hoodie.

The young woman opened the back door and shouted. "I have a fare for you!"

Evelyn's pulse kicked up a notch, and she couldn't help but wonder if it would be her Uncle Yazzie.

His had been the only taxi cab in town twenty years ago. When her father had been working endless hours at the clinic, or in Juneau at the hospital, Uncle Yazzie would come and pick her up every day in his taxi cab and take her to school. She'd often stay with him and her grandmother. Her mother's people.

A young man of about twenty, who looked very familiar, came out from the back.

He beamed at her and held out his hand. "Can I take you someplace, miss?"

She didn't answer as she racked her brain for how she knew this man.

"Are you okay, miss?" he asked, appearing slightly uncomfortable with her staring.

"Sorry, you look so familiar," she said, before catching herself.

"Really? I look like my dad—or so they tell me."

"Then it must be jet lag messing with me." She rubbed her eyes. "I didn't mean to gawk at you. Just déjà vu."

The young man smiled. "It happens. Don't worry. Unless you know my dad?"

"Who is your dad?" she asked.

"Joe—Yazzie Sr. I'm Joe Jr. Do you know him?"

Evelyn's heart skipped a beat as she saw it now. Saw the younger version of her uncle in this young man. Obviously Uncle Yazzie's son had been born after she'd left. For a moment she had a pang of homesickness. She'd missed Joe Jr.'s birth. Her *cousin's* birth.

Evelyn's heart stopped its racing and she took his hand. "The name sounds familiar…"

She wasn't lying—she just wasn't telling him the whole story. There would be time for that later...that was if his father was interested in seeing her again.

"Not surprising. He doesn't leave Wolf's Harbor."

"Well, I'm Dr. Evelyn Saunders. I'm looking for a ride to the medical clinic."

"Of course—you're the new OB/GYN in town for the next three months, yeah?" He picked up her suitcase.

"I am," Evelyn answered.

"My wife..." He pointed over his shoulder at the young woman behind the counter. "Jennifer—she's due in a month."

Jennifer beamed and nodded. "I have an appointment with you tomorrow afternoon, Dr. Saunders."

"Well, I look forward to seeing you then."

Evelyn quickly reassessed the small bump under her hoodie and some red flags went up. It could be nothing. Some woman were known to carry very small until right near the end. But Evelyn would be sure to check out Jennifer Yazzie's file as soon as she got access to the patient records.

She followed Joe Jr. out of the terminal and to a blue and orange cab that was painted exactly the same as the old cab she remembered, but a new model of the vehicle.

She slipped into the passenger seat in the front and after Joe had got her luggage in the back he took the driver's seat and started the cab.

"Is this your first time in Wolf's Harbor, Dr. Saunders?"

"No." She wanted to say yes—to serve her three-month rotation and maybe go unnoticed, so she could leave the painful memories of her past behind her—but she couldn't lie.

She'd lost a piece of herself when she'd been taken away from Wolf's Harbor, and even though she was only going to be here for a short time perhaps she could lay to rest some of the ghosts that continued to haunt her. Stop the restless feeling she often got. The night terrors which sometimes still plagued her.

"Really?" Joe asked. "I don't remember seeing your face before."

"How old are you, Joe?" she asked.

"Twenty—which I know is young to be a father..."

"I wasn't going to judge you for your age, or

tell you that you're too young to be a father—it's just that the last time I was in Wolf's Harbor I was ten, which was twenty years ago."

Joe beamed. "No kidding? Well, welcome home."

He didn't pry further, for which she was glad, but she was sure that he'd soon be getting the word out that she was back.

It would be better this way. To let everyone know that she had come back instead of facing a constant stream of questioning shock. She just hoped they wouldn't all give her the cold shoulder as they had done for the past twenty years.

Twenty years with no word from her family up here.

Twenty years of silence.

Joe pulled up in front of the clinic and she paid the fare, insisting that he keep the change. The clinic was a new building with red siding. It reminded her of a barn, but it was very clean, with the sign freshly painted. It sat on the main road downtown, and through the gaps in the buildings across from her she could see the tall masts and onboard hoists of the fishing boats in the harbor. Her father had practiced medicine out of a small storefront. This looked so much better than that cramped old space.

Joe set her luggage down beside her.

"I guess I'll see you tomorrow, Dr. Saunders."

Evelyn grinned. "See you tomorrow, Joe."

She picked up her luggage as Joe drove away. The clinic sign said "Closed" and there was no sign of Dr. Pearson anywhere. It began to drizzle and Evelyn tried the handle. The door was unlocked and she stepped inside.

There was no nurse behind the reception desk. It was quiet. Deserted.

Great.

She wandered past the reception desk, looking for someone. Anyone.

"Dr. Pearson?" she called out. She was met with only silence.

Just great.

She peeked into an exam room and flicked on the light. It was modern and well stocked, which surprised her for such a small community. She wandered through the room, taking it all in. She couldn't believe that she was back here. Back in Wolf's Harbor.

Home.

Evelyn cursed under her breath. She had to stop thinking about this place as her home. This was not her home. It hadn't been for some time.

Still, it was hard not to think of those days. And all the time that had been taken away from her.

And whose fault was that?

"Who are you?" a harsh voice demanded.

Evelyn spun round and was taken aback by the sight of the most handsome man she'd ever seen. She felt a bit stunned, and all she could do was stare at him in awe. He was tall, broad-shouldered. He wore a flannel shirt stretched a little tight over his strong, muscular upper arms. His dark hair was close-cropped and his skin was a warm, deep tawny brown. He had a neatly kept beard. But it was his eyes, a green-gray-blue, which were really stunning. Clear, bright—and focused on *her*.

They held her rooted to the spot.

"You're not supposed to be in here," he growled.

"Are you Dr. Pearson?" she asked, finally finding her voice.

His eyes narrowed. "No. He's gone back to Juneau."

"What?" Evelyn frowned. "You've got to be kidding me!"

* * *

Derek had been in the back. He had been waiting for the new doctor to arrive, annoyed that Dr. Pearson had left for Juneau early and saddled him with the new OB/GYN when he had a full caseload as general practitioner to handle.

He hadn't left for a bigger city even though he could have.

His mother had begged him to return to Chicago when Vivian died. She'd even offered to retire from her catering business to help him raise his daughter, but he couldn't leave Alaska.

He might have been born in Chicago but, like his parents—one of whom came from Haiti and one from the Ukraine—he needed to forge his own path. Put down his own roots. And Wolf's Harbor had been the place to do that.

He loved it here. Loved the people. Loved his life.

Even though as a widower it was slightly lonely. *Whose fault is that?*

It had been his choice to be alone after his wife had died from a uterine rupture when their daughter was born. His life was his practice and his daughter.

Still, he was annoyed that he had to deal with

these rotating doctors. Doctors who came in and left him with more work in the end. Doctors who saw the patients of Wolf's Harbor as an inconvenience. He was tired of the extra burden, but he'd gladly bear it for his patients.

Dr. Pearson had left him high and dry by leaving before the new OB/GYN showed up, and Mo was still getting over a bug she'd picked up, so he had to relieve the sitter. He would be glad when school started again. He had no time to deal with another rotation doctor and Dr. Pearson had just dumped this one in his lap.

So like Dr. Pearson. So like *all* these doctors who came through the town, never staying longer than they had too. Never willing to help him out or put in a good word to get a hospital built in town. These big city doctors were all selfish—if it wouldn't further their career they didn't lend a hand.

Okay, you're sounding like a curmudgeon now.

He stuck it out all year in this isolated community, while these specialists fluttered in and out, never staying long enough to get to know the people. There was no real trust between these doctors and the patients. It was a dangerous thing.

He tried not to think about how the lack of a

specialist during one of these rotations had cost him everything. How his late wife had hemorrhaged and bled out before they could get her on an air ambulance to Sitka. And the fact that it had happened during a storm that had grounded all the planes had made it so much worse. There had been nothing he could do. But if there had been a hospital here in Wolf's Harbor maybe she would have had a fighting chance.

He focused on this fiery, auburn-haired woman, who thought it was okay just to waltz into his closed office. He'd been taken back by the beautiful, tall, polished woman who was now standing in his exam room. *So* like Dr. Pearson to have his girlfriends and paramours just show up unannounced.

Although he was a bit jealous that this one was one of Dr. Pearson's girlfriends…

He'd seen many of them go through this clinic when Dr. Pearson had been here on rotation, but this one—this one actually made him jealous of Dr. Pearson.

It had been a long time since he'd been attracted to someone. If he didn't have Mo, or the practice to run—if he was the same man he had been before he'd come to Wolf's Harbor—he would pursue a woman just like this.

You're lonely. Face it.

"Pearson has gone back to Juneau," Derek said again, and moved from the doorway to encourage her to leave. "Sorry for your trouble. I can call you a cab…"

"I'm the new OB/GYN. I'm Dr. Saunders."

Derek frowned. "What? I thought that this was Dr. Merritt's rotation?"

"Dr. Merritt just went on an extended honeymoon," Dr. Saunders said. "I'm covering her practice."

"What?" Derek asked, scowling. So now Dr. Merritt had just got a replacement without consulting him? Not that Dr. Merritt *had* to consult him, but it would have been considerate of her to do so.

At least she sent someone else.

Although he knew nothing about this Dr. Saunders. "Well, that's unacceptable. Just because we're a small town, it doesn't mean we'll take *anyone*."

She crossed her arms. "Why is it unacceptable?"

"I know nothing about you."

"So?" she replied firmly. "You need an OB/ GYN and there are appointments tomorrow."

"How do you know there are appointments to-morrow? You obviously don't know Dr. Pearson, because you thought I was him."

"First, I know there are appointments here to-morrow because Joe Yazzie Jr. and his wife are expected for prenatal. I introduced myself to them when I landed from Sitka. And second I assumed you were a doctor—was I mistaken?"

The nerve of her.

Of course he was pleased that she'd already made a connection with one of his patients. She had one up on every other doctor who'd waltzed through here.

But why were redheads always like this? Every one he'd ever encountered in Chicago had been like this. And of course he was a complete sucker for them.

You can't have her.

He had to keep reminding himself of that fact. He wanted nothing to do with someone who would leave after her rotation was done. He wanted nothing to do with *anyone* ever again.

Not since Vivian had died.

He was not going to go through anything like

that again. Besides, he had Mo to think of, and his practice, his patients. That was what was important.

"I *am* a doctor," he said tersely. "I'm the general practitioner of Wolf's Harbor."

"Are you on rotation too?" she asked.

"No," he snapped. "Unlike you and Dr. Pearson, I am here all the time. Wolf's Harbor is my home. I actually *care* about my patients and their medical care enough to stay."

Her eyes narrowed and a strange expression crossed her face, but only briefly.

"If you truly cared about your patients then you wouldn't object to me being here. I'm here to stay."

His eyes widened. He was surprised. "Stay? As in permanently?"

She blushed. "Well…no."

Of course not. He knew better than to get his hopes up.

Who was this woman?

"I'm just as capable as Dr. Merritt," she said, breaking the tension.

"Are you?" he asked, raising an eyebrow. "I at least *know* Dr. Merritt. I know nothing about you. Not even your first name."

She smiled tightly. "Dr. Evelyn Saunders. I just completed my fellowship in fetal surgery at Richler Medicine in Seattle. I'm one of the few people in this country who can perform delicate fetal surgeries. I'm also a board-certified obstetrical and gynecological fellow, and a pediatric fellow specializing in premature infants. I completed that fellowship and practiced for three years at the Mayo Clinic in Rochester, Minnesota. You can check my credentials, but they speak for themselves. I am more experienced than Dr. Merritt and I will be an asset to your patients."

Damn. She was right.

And he was completely impressed by her résumé and where she'd studied. She had every right to be confident to the point of obnoxiousness.

She was a triple threat and he'd be an absolute idiot to turn her away—but he couldn't help but wonder why someone with so much experience didn't have a thriving practice of her own.

Who cares? She can help your patients even if it's only for a short time.

He couldn't help but wonder if someone like her had been here that horrific night five years ago Vivian would still be here and he wouldn't be alone. Mo would have her mother. He'd still have that piece of his heart and soul that had been torn away the night he'd lost Vivian. The night Mo had lost her mother. His patients needed her.

"Fine." He sighed and he ran a hand over his head. "I'll show you to the apartment and get you a clinic key, then give you all the information you need to start tomorrow."

"Thank you, Dr…?" she asked, extending a hand.

"Dr. Taylor. Dr. Derek Taylor." He ignored her hand, afraid to touch her and still not wanting her to feel too welcome. "Come on, I'll show you to your place."

His mother would *totally* be slapping him upside the head if she could see how he was being such a jerk to this woman, but he couldn't get attached. Dr. Saunders would be gone in three months and he had no interest in getting attached to someone who wasn't going to stick it out for the long run.

It was so much easier on his heart this way. Better for Mo too. He didn't want her to get hurt. He'd promised Vivian he'd protect Mo. So he planned to treat Evelyn like every other physician who passed through Wolf's Harbor on rotation. Even if she *was* easy on the eye and had a spirited personality—the kind which always drew him in when it came to members of the opposite sex...

He was a professional above all else. His patients came first. And even though he knew nothing about her—even though training a new doctor about the ins and outs of Wolf's Harbor Medical would be an extra burden on him—he'd gladly do it.

Unlike all the other doctors who came and went, *he* was here for the long haul.

CHAPTER TWO

HE'S A BIT cool and stand-offish.

Evelyn waited outside with her rolling suitcase as Dr. Taylor—Derek—locked up the clinic. It was beginning to drizzle and it was dusk, but since it was summer it would stay light pretty late.

She glanced at her watch and remembered she hadn't switched it over to Alaska daylight time.

Derek whistled. "That's some fancy watch you have there!"

Heat bloomed in her cheeks, because she'd caught the undertone of his sarcasm. Yeah it was flashy and out of place here, but he didn't have to point it out. "It was my grandmother's. She left it to me when she passed."

His expression softened. "Sorry."

"She had a good life. She was ninety-nine when I lost her to cancer. I miss her—she was the only family I had."

No, she wasn't, a little whisper said in her mind,

but she ignored it. She knew now that Uncle Yazzie was still around, but Léelk'w probably wasn't. Still, she'd been gone for twenty years and had had no contact with any of them. It was apparent that they hadn't thought of her. Joe Jr. hadn't even blinked an eye when she'd told him her last name.

So she had no family left. Not really.

"I understand," he muttered, but then shook his head as if he felt bad about what he'd said. "Look, let's get out of this drizzle before it turns to full-out rain."

"That's fine with me. Is the apartment far?"

"Nope." Derek shoved his hands in his hoodie and headed up an alleyway behind the clinic.

Evelyn rolled her eyes and followed him. It wasn't really an alleyway after all, but a steep slope up to a set of wooden stairs that were at the back of the clinic.

"This is the place," Derek said. "There's no connection to the clinic on the inside, however."

"Great—well, at least it's summer." Evelyn would hate to climb those open wooden steps to the second floor in the winter. She wouldn't be here then.

A shudder ran down her spine as she thought

of those cold Alaska nights. How the sun had set early, the northern lights had shone and there had been hot chocolate by the fire with her father in the cabin.

He had read to her for hours, until her eyes were so heavy that he'd had to carry her to bed and tuck her in while the snowstorms had raged outside her window.

She'd been safe in her father's arms.

"Come on, then," Derek said, interrupting her thoughts as he jogged up the steps, not even offering to take her suitcase for her.

Evelyn cursed under her breath and lugged the case up, bumping it with each step. So much for her new luggage.

At the top Derek was waiting, and he was smirking. She wanted to wipe it off his face.

"You okay there?" he asked, a hint of humor in his voice.

"Perfectly," Evelyn said through gritted teeth.

Derek opened the door and stepped inside. She dragged her suitcase in. The apartment was a mess.

Derek was annoyed. "Yeah, sorry about this. I forgot. Dr. Pearson is a bit of a slob."

"It's fine," Evelyn said. She could clean it up,

no problem. She was definitely not a fan of Dr. Pearson, though. First the jerk had left without waiting for her, leaving her to the mercy of Dr. Derek Taylor, and now this.

Derek handed her a key ring. "The clinic key is this large one and the other is the apartment."

"Is there a car that's available for me while I'm here?"

"Unless you drove one in from the ferry terminal that connects to Juneau then, no, but everything is in walking distance."

Great.

She'd been hoping a car would be available because she wanted to see if her father's place was still standing. She was wondering if it had changed. From going through what had been left to her after her grandmother had died, she knew that the property had been sold shortly after she'd left Wolf's Harbor.

Grandma hadn't want any part of Wolf's Harbor. She hadn't wanted any reminders of her son's worst mistake.

"Your father could've been a great surgeon, but he left for Alaska and took up with your mother and I never saw him again. He could've been great, Evelyn, but he threw it all away for

a woman who was not part of the world he was brought up in."

Evelyn shook her grandmother's voice from her head.

Her father might not have become the kind of surgical god her grandmother always envisioned, but he'd been a respected general practitioner in Wolf's Harbor. People had looked up to him. He'd saved lives and her grandmother had never got to see it.

Now she, Evelyn, would finish what he'd started and lay the memories of her father to rest. Maybe then she could move on.

"I flew in from Sitka," she said as she pocketed the keys. "So if I want to order in a pizza I just say the back of the clinic?"

"Yeah—they'll know," Derek said. "The clinic opens at nine."

"And how do I access patients' records? Is there a computer password?"

"No password—and you can access the patients' records by opening the filing cabinet. Your schedule is on the receptionist's calendar."

There was that smug sense of humor again. As if he was trying to shock her with the fact that they still had hard copies of their records.

"Okay. Well, I'll be there earlier than nine to get myself acquainted with everything."

Derek reached out, grabbing the arm with the fancy watch, and stared at its face. "Not if you don't set your alarm to Alaska Daylight Savings, you won't."

Just that simple touch caused a shiver of anticipation to run down her spine. He was annoying, but there was something about him which drew her in.

He was dangerous.

She had no interest in any relationship. Every relationship she'd been in had ended with her being dumped because she could never commit—because she was never there and was too focused on her career. Or so those men had believed. She'd actually pushed them away because she knew she didn't deserve what she secretly wanted.

A family of her own.

She shook him off. "I'm well aware of the time-change."

He smirked and raised an eyebrow, then moved past her through the open door. "Okay, then. I'll see you tomorrow—bright and early. Good night, Dr. Saunders."

Evelyn shut the door after him and was glad to be rid of him. For now.

She'd see him tomorrow, but after a good night's rest she knew that she would be better suited to dealing with him.

She could handle guys like Derek. Guys who were arrogant and used to being the lone wolf. They saw every new arrival as a threat.

Nathan had been nothing like Derek. When she'd first met him he'd been nice and almost too accommodating. Still, look where that had got her. It had got her nowhere. She'd spent two years of her life with Nathan and he'd left her.

You really gave him nothing, though. Remember?

She locked the door and scrubbed a hand over her face, staring at the apartment and feeling completely exhausted and hungry.

There was a clock that was showing Alaska time, so she quickly set her watch even as her stomach growled, reminding her that she hadn't had much to eat since leaving Sitka. While she'd been dragging her bag up the stairs she'd noticed a pub across the road, and it had looked like the kind of bar that might serve a quick meal. She was starving. She didn't feel like waiting for pizza. She felt antsy, trapped in this messy apartment. It would be better for her to get out of there and grab a breath of fresh air.

She grabbed her purse and her keys. First she'd eat and then she'd tackle this mess—even though she was still running on East Coast time and needed to sleep.

The drizzle had dissipated and a damp mist hung in the air. Outside it was quiet, with only a couple of trucks slowly puttering through down town. She knew that it was at least three hours to the nearest ferry terminal, and then four hours to Juneau. Wolf's Harbor was remote, and sur-rounded by the dense, mountainous forests of the Inside Passage.

She remembered when her father had used to drive her to the far side of the island, to the ferry terminal, so she could watch the large ferry bringing people to the island and sometimes a cruise ship on its way to Skagway. And some-times she'd see the orcas.

For the most part Wolf's Harbor relied on log-ging and fishing, and it was only fishing vessels or large logging trucks that would go by.

A shiver ran down her spine as she thought of her father's death. How he'd been hit by that runaway logging truck that had been going too fast through town. And how a ring had been in his pocket.

"Evelyn, your mother has been gone a long time now. Jocelyn isn't going to replace her. She makes me happy. Be good. I won't be long at Jocelyn's."

That had been the last time she'd seen her father alive. The last words he'd said.

Don't think about it.

She dashed across the road and straight into the pub.

As soon as she took a step inside the murmur of hushed talking stopped and people stared at her. There'd never been a lot of visitors when she was a kid.

"Hi," she said, waving uneasily. "I'm the new doctor in town."

There was another few seconds of stares, which felt like an eternity, but then most people returned to their food, their conversations or their drinks.

Except one.

Derek.

He was positively glowering at her from the far side of the bar. And he was next to the only empty seat in the place.

Great.

Maybe it would be better to wait for pizza? But of course now that she'd made her entrance and he was staring at her she couldn't really back down.

So she pretended to ignore him and sat down, picking up one of the vinyl-covered menus and pretending to study it, ignoring the sensation of his staring at her.

"I thought you would be cleaning," Derek said gruffly.

She glanced at him. "Usually a gentleman would introduce himself or offer to buy a woman a drink before trying to strike up a conversation with her."

Derek snickered, staring ahead at the bar. She could see his reflection in the mirror.

"I'm no gentleman. And you know who I am."

"Do I?" she muttered.

He got up and just stood there, saying nothing until she turned and looked at him.

"What?" she asked.

"Hi, I'm Derek Taylor. Can I buy you a drink?"

"Not interested." And she turned back to her menu, trying not to smile.

"Oh, for the love of…"

"Sit down." She chuckled. "I don't need a drink."

Derek sat down, setting his mug of beer back on the bar. "I'm surprised to see you out and about."

"Why is that?" she asked.

"Because usually the specialists who come into town to do their rotation don't bother with the locals. They order in, keep to themselves—it's somewhat of a burden."

"Well, the cleaning of that apartment is 'somewhat of a burden.'"

She set down the menu. She was hungry, but she wasn't sure she really wanted to eat at this moment. Her stomach was twisting and turning from being back here. And as she glanced around the dim bar she had faint memories of this place.

Her father and Uncle Yazzie playing pool here, and her mother singing up on that stage. Her last gig before she'd got sick with the cancer that had killed her. And as she studied the room further she remembered the booth that was reserved for live entertainment. It had seemed so much bigger when she'd been curled up in it, eating ice cream.

"Daddy, what're you doing?" Evelyn asked, seeing her father with another woman.

Her dad stood up, shocked. "Evie, what're you doing here?"

Her eyes brimmed with tears. "I saw your truck outside. I was running an errand for Léelk'w. Who is that woman?"

"This is Jocelyn. She's my girlfriend."

Jocelyn smiled and waved. She was pretty, blonde and young—and not her mother.

"No!" Evelyn screamed. "No!"

And she turned and ran out of the bar.

Her father yelled for her to come back.

"Hey, you okay?" Derek asked, interrupting her memory.

"Yeah," she said, and ran her hand through her hair in the nervous twitch she'd always had. "Yeah, I'm fine."

"You totally zoned out," Derek said. "Tired?"

"A bit."

"Where did you say you were from?" he asked, trying to draw her into conversation.

"Boston, but I've been in Sitka a couple of days."

"Still, the change is a bit jarring if you're not used to it."

"I'm used to it," she whispered. "It's just been a long time."

Derek cocked an eyebrow. "Pardon?"

The door opened and the hair on the back of her neck stood on end. She slowly turned around in her seat, because instinctively she knew what to expect and she wasn't sure she was ready for it.

She wasn't ready to face a ghost from her past.

Taking a deep breath, she stood and looked up at the man who had been her family. A man she'd never thought she'd see again because her grandmother had cut off all ties to Evelyn's life here in Alaska.

The man her father had thought of as a brother, because he had estranged himself from his WASP mother back in Boston, "throwing his life away" to live in the wilderness.

It had been Uncle Yazzie who had introduced her parents. Her mother's loveable, goofball little brother. A man who had represented everything her grandmother had hated about her son's life and his wife in Alaska.

Tears stung her eyes as she stared into the dark eyes of Joe Yazzie Sr. She could still see him standing on the Tarmac of the airport all those years ago when she'd been forced to move to Boston.

"I had to see with my own eyes," Yazzie whispered. "I thought my son was bluffing me."

Her stomach twisted into a knot as she wondered if he would turn his back on her. She wanted to run. She was afraid of his rejection in person, because his silence had hurt her as a child.

No. You have to face him. Good or bad.

"Uncle Yazzie…" she whispered, her voice faltering.

Derek was highly confused. "What's going on here?"

Evelyn sighed and turned back to Derek. "I'm from Wolf's Harbor. I'm a local."

She's a local?

If Evelyn Saunders was a local he would know that. He'd lived here for fifteen years and he knew everyone in this town because he was the general practitioner.

And he would remember her.

She was local?

He was still in a bit of disbelief over it all, but there was no denying it when he saw Joe Yazzie Sr.'s reaction to her.

The man who was usually stone-cold and emotionless had his arms wrapped around her, holding her and crying.

Crying?

Derek did a double-take. He'd never seen Joe Sr. cry. *Ever.*

"Am I missing something?" Derek asked.

Joe took a step back, tears glistening in his eyes as he spoke some words in Tlingit.

Derek could only make out a piece of what he was saying. Something about someone being home?

Joe turned to him. "Dr. Taylor, this is my sister's child. She's been missing for over twenty years."

"Missing?" Derek asked, confused.

Evelyn smiled up at Joe and then looked back at Derek. "My father died when I was ten and my guardian was my grandmother in Boston. A social worker came and—"

"Took her away," Joe interrupted. "We were her family. Her father left her care to me and my mother. Evelyn is half-Tlingit and we would've cared for her, but we lost out to the Matriarch Saunders in Boston. There was no will, and a judge determined Georgina Saunders a better fit. She had the finances...we didn't and couldn't afford to fight. Georgina had sole custody. It broke my mother's heart, being separated from her. We tried to call, but Georgina changed her number and blocked us at every turn."

"I see." Derek was in shock.

Joe turned back to Evelyn. "We tried to get in touch with you, Evie. I swear!"

Evelyn nodded, only Derek noticed a strange expression on her face, as if she didn't quite believe it. "I know."

"So you're related to the Yazzie family? You didn't mention it before," Derek said.

Evelyn shot him a warning look. "It didn't come up naturally in conversation."

"I asked where you were from."

"I am from Boston."

Joe frowned. "Well, I'm glad you're back, Evie. We have a lot to catch up on."

"I think that's my cue to go," Derek said as he stood up.

"You don't have to," Evelyn said.

"I have things to do. I'll see you tomorrow." He quickly slapped down money for his beer.

He had to get out of this place. He had to put some distance between him and Evelyn. *Fast.* He'd overstayed anyways. He'd only come for a quick drink before he had to head home to relieve the sitter and deal with a cranky, fussy five-year-old who wanted the sitter to stay longer because Jessica read stories better than Daddy.

Derek looked back at the reunion scene. He smiled and for one brief moment wished he could stay. Evelyn's smile made his heart skip a beat. It made him feel like his old self.

Seeing Evelyn with Joe Yazzie made him feel lonely.

She was from here.

She had family.

He frowned at the realization.

Evelyn had a reason to stay, and if she stayed…

He didn't want to get his hopes up that another doctor would stay. They never did. So he was going to carry on believing she was like every other doctor before her. A doctor with a time limit.

Even if secretly he wouldn't mind if she stayed, because he was so drawn to her and it would be nice to share the load—

That thought scared him.

There was no room in his heart for anyone else.

His heart was too broken, too damaged, for him to make room for someone again.

CHAPTER THREE

EVELYN GOT UP before her alarm in the morning. Of course it had been hard to sleep, because her emotions were all over the place.

The reunion with Uncle Yazzie had wrung her out completely, even if she *had* managed to keep it all together. And every time she'd closed her eyes she'd seen her father, her mother or Derek. And the fact that Derek had invaded her thoughts irritated her greatly.

He shouldn't be in her thoughts.

She was here to serve Stefanie's rotation in Wolf's Harbor and then she'd return to Sitka. And then… She didn't know where.

There were so many opportunities.

Nathan hadn't understood that about her. She wanted to keep learning and expanding her curriculum vitae. She wanted to learn from the very best in her field of work. And all Nathan had wanted to do was stay put, have kids and settle down.

You want those things too. You're just afraid.

Evelyn ignored those thoughts. They were dangerous to have, and she was never going to entertain them. She was never going to have a husband or kids. She didn't want to put her heart at risk or, worse, have her kids go through the traumatic experience that she had.

Evelyn swore she would never do that. Even if she wanted it badly.

"You're restless, Evelyn."

Nathan's words echoed in her head.

Maybe she was, but she could protect herself better this way.

She took a sip of the instant coffee she'd made from the powder she'd found in a cupboard and winced.

It was awful. Bitter.

She dumped the coffee down the sink before gathering up her things and heading outside. She shivered, even though it was summer. It was brisk compared to Boston, and she was glad she'd brought her sweater.

Down the steps and through the alleyway beside the clinic was a small coffee shop, and she could smell coffee brewing.

The bell above the door jingled as she walked in and a sudden rush of being there before, washed over her. The scent of coffee and the sugary sweet smell of pies wafted in from the back.

She'd been here before, but she was having a hard time remembering it.

A middle-aged woman looked up from cleaning the counter and beamed. "Well, I'll be…"

"Hi," Evelyn said unsurely.

"Joe told me that you had come home."

The woman came out from behind the counter and before Evelyn could stop her she was being wrapped up in the woman's arms and crushed in a bear hug.

"You don't remember me, do you?" the woman asked, her smile not disappearing.

"No, I'm sorry."

"That's okay." The proprietor walked back behind the counter. "You left so long ago. Your father used to come in here every day to get coffee. I'm Sally."

Evelyn smiled at Sally. "Nice to meet you… again."

Sally grinned. "No worries. What will it be, Evie…? I mean, Dr. Saunders. *That's* going to be hard for me to get used to saying. I can't believe you're a doctor. Your dad would be so proud."

Just the simple mention of her father caused

Evelyn a pang of longing. And then the memory came back to her.

Yellow curtains filtering in the bright sunlight on those odd days when the sun would peek through the clouds. Chocolate milk and her father blowing the steam across the top of his coffee before he took a sip. And *her*. That woman Jocelyn with her bright smile and golden hair. The one who'd tried to take her mother's place.

Evelyn shook the memory away. She had to focus on today.

"Can I have a coffee, please?"

"Of course, Dr. Saunders." Sally turned and picked up a carafe of coffee. It smelled heavenly. "Would you like it to go?"

"Yes, that would be great, Sally."

Evelyn took a seat at the counter, her pulse thundering in her ears because nothing had changed. The drapes were faded, but everything was the same. She'd forgotten about this place, but the moment Sally had mentioned her father it had come flooding back to her.

And the pain was just as raw as it had been twenty years ago.

She hated feeling it again.

You knew this would be hard. That's why you're here.

The door chimed again and Derek walked in, pulling down the hood of his hoodie.

"Brisk out there today, Sally. Can I get…?" He trailed off as those brilliant gray-green eyes locked onto her, sending a shiver of the dreams from the night before through her.

His eyes were the most intense she'd ever seen.

"Good morning," she said, breaking the gaze so she could look away and try not to let him see her blush by hiding behind her long hair.

"Good morning," Derek said carefully, and took the stool next to her at the counter. "I see you got up early."

"I told you that I would." She held out her arm and pointed to her watch. "See—it's set on Alaska time."

A brief smile flitted across Derek's face. "So it is."

"And I have my key. So I'm not going to be a burden for you."

Sally handed her a coffee. "There you go, Dr. Saunders."

"Thanks, Sally. How much do I owe you?"

Sally shook her head. "Not today. It's on the house. A welcome back gift from me."

"Thank you!"

"Hey, I've been your physician for fifteen years—how come *I* don't get a free coffee every now and again?" Derek complained.

Sally frowned. "You're not local."

"I've been here longer than *she* has," Derek teased.

Evelyn playfully stuck out her tongue and beamed at Sally. "I'll see you later, Sally. Thanks for the coffee."

She felt like skipping out of that coffee shop, but she refrained.

She didn't get very far before Derek, carrying his own paper cup, came jogging up beside her. "You won over Sally pretty fast," he said, sounding impressed. "Not many people do."

"She seems cheerful enough."

Derek's eyes narrowed. "She knows you—but you don't remember her, do you?"

"I told her that," Evelyn said. "I was young when I left. Are you telling me she's usually a grump?"

Derek frowned and took a pull of his coffee.

"Maybe she's only a grump with me. She said once that she didn't like doctors."

"I hate to break it to you, but *I'm* a doctor," she said lightly.

"Yeah, but you're Thorne Saunders' daughter, and those who remember you have a warm fuzzy feeling when it comes to you. Which will change when you leave again."

"What's that supposed to mean?" Evelyn asked as Derek sidestepped her to open the door of the clinic. "And how do you know my father's name? I never told you."

"Come on—you're not going to be here forever, Saunders," he said as he stepped through the door and flicked on the fluorescent lights. "It's just a phase. And I did some research last night. Your father was the first general practitioner to stay in Wolf's Harbor. He was the first to stay and help the people here. I'm impressed."

That gave her a punch in the gut that she hadn't been expecting, because he was right. They remembered her father with fondness, but really they were just being kind. These weren't *her* people.

She'd been gone too long.

And you're the reason why your father's dead.

"I'm just here to do my job. I can't control people's reactions to me. But if I instill some kind of trust in them while I'm here, then all the better."

"Don't get your feathers ruffled," Derek said as he set his coffee cup on the counter. "I'm just stating a fact."

"Yeah, because you're annoyed by the townspeople's reaction to me. My guess is they never really warm up to the other doctors that rotate through here. Am I right? And that gives you some sort of power."

Those intense eyes flickered with something close to anger and she realized she'd struck a nerve.

Good.

"You have use of exam rooms three and four. One and two are mine for today." He picked up his coffee cup and stormed away to the first exam room.

Evelyn was going to ask him more when the clinic's door chimed and a young woman in scrubs came in, stopping dead in her tracks as she looked up at Evelyn.

"Oh, you're not Dr. Merritt," she said.

Evelyn sighed and plastered a fake smile on her face, bracing herself to explain who she was again. Hopefully the nurse wouldn't gave the same contempt for her that Derek did, but she wasn't going to hold her breath just yet.

Derek had been managing to avoid Evelyn all morning, but to give her credit she was taking good care of her patients and they genuinely looked happy to see her. Or at least that was what Janet, his nurse and current spy, had said.

He picked up the next file in his pile.

Great.

He always had trouble with this patient, and he couldn't even begin to think why she was here today.

"Katlian Yazzie?"

The venerable old woman stood up and fixed him with a stare that meant business. "Well, it's about time. I'm not getting any younger."

Derek tried not to roll his eyes—and then a thought crept through his head. If Evelyn was related to Mrs. Yazzie's son Joe, then she was probably familiar with Katlian Yazzie. For one brief moment he thought about palming her off on Evelyn.

Mrs. Yazzie made it clear time and time again that she didn't trust doctors. *"I like you, Dr. Tay-*

lor. I just don't trust you. I don't trust any of you."
And he couldn't help but wonder if she'd trusted
Thorne Saunders. Most had.

Thorne was a bit of legend. He had been the
first doctor to stay and after his death no one had
stayed. Not until *he* came.

Of course the Yazzies didn't speak of Thorne
the way the other locals did, and now he understood why. Thorne had been family, and he understood how grief could devastate. How it was
too painful to talk and just easier to bottle it up.

"It's good to see you again," Derek said, grin-
ning at her.

"Don't *even!*" she teased. "I know you're not
thrilled to see me, but I'm not here to see *you*.
I'm here to see the OB/GYN. This Dr. Merritt."

"Dr. Merritt isn't here, Katlian."

"Joe Jr.'s wife is supposed to see her this afternoon and I wanted to talk to her about Jennifer's
birthing plan. I didn't trust that Dr. Pearson."

"That I can agree with you on, but Dr. Merritt
got married and sent in a replacement. Have you
talked to your son?" he asked gently.

Katlian's brow furrowed. "What does it matter
if I talked to Joe. He knows nothing. Why would

I…?" The words died in her throat as Evelyn stepped out of one of the examination rooms.

Evelyn wasn't paying attention to them at first—she was flipping through a file before she stepped back into the exam room. Not even noticing them.

Katlian turned away and covered her mouth with her hand. She'd gone pale, as if she'd seen a ghost.

Derek reached out and held her shoulders, steadying her. "That's why I was wondering if you'd talked to your son."

"Is that…?" Katlian's voice wavered.

"Dr. Evelyn Saunders," Derek answered. Then he guided Katlian toward exam room number one, away from some of the curious onlookers in the waiting room. He helped Katlian take a seat and then shut the door.

Katlian was wide-eyed. "I haven't talked to Joe since the day before yesterday. I've been staying with Joe Jr. and Jennifer. They didn't tell me."

"Joe Jr. didn't know who Dr. Saunders was. But I think he told his father, because Joe Sr. and Dr. Saunders had a reunion last night."

He'd seen the love there in Joe Sr.'s eyes when he'd looked at Evelyn, but he'd seen fear in hers.

The way she'd held herself, her body rigid, her smile fixed—she had been throwing up walls.

Derek knew the art of going through the motions. He'd practiced that art so many times after Vivian had died, when all people had done was offer him condolences and feel sorry for him. What he'd needed was help. So he'd learned to put on that act. Worn that armor to shield his heart from pain.

He wondered why Evelyn felt she needed to do that.

What had happened when her parents died?

He knew she'd been taken away, but there must be more to the story.

Is it really your business?

No, it wasn't and he was annoyed with himself for caring so much, but for some reason he couldn't help himself when it came to Evelyn.

She drew him in. Just this short time of getting to know her and he was completely drawn to her. He wanted to know more about her, and that was a dangerous thing indeed.

Katlian Yazzie smiled. "Evie's mother was my daughter. Evie…"

Katlian wept.

Derek was taken aback by the usually stoic

woman's crying and was at a loss as to what to do. He slipped his arm around the old woman. "Joe mentioned she was taken away?"

Katlian nodded. "By Thorne's mother. Because a judge deemed that *she* was better for Evelyn. That Boston was better than Wolf's Harbor."

"Why would a judge decide that? Evelyn knew Wolf's Harbor not Boston," said Derek.

"Because Boston had access to more healthcare. Thorne was our only doctor… Well, you know no one replaced him after he died. Not until you came. So the judge decided in favor of Boston and not here."

Derek's stomach twisted in a knot. He understood that. If there had been a local hospital on the day of that storm that had grounded all the planes to Sitka, Vivian would have had a chance of survival, instead of bleeding to death.

"Thorne died at the scene—no hospital could've saved him. Joe and I fought. We fought hard—spent money that we didn't have—but we lost. We didn't have the money or the power that Georgina Saunders in Boston had. We had to walk away. I wrote to Evie constantly, but my letters were returned to sender. Once Joe went down there to see her, but Georgina had taken Evelyn away on a long vacation so he had to come back. Georgina had sole custody. We had nothing."

"I'm sure if you explain…"

Katlian sighed. "I need a moment."

"Do you still want to talk to her about Jennifer?"

Katlian shook her head. "I don't know if she would want to see me. I don't know if I'm ready to see her or even if she'll remember me."

Derek was moved by Katlian Yazzie. There was a heart in there. Everyone in Wolf's Harbor loved Katlian Yazzie, even Mo, but with Derek she'd always been untrusting and a bit cold. This was a different side to her.

"She's a doctor!" Katlian said in disbelief. "A doctor!"

"Maybe you'll have to change your stance on doctors now, eh?" he teased.

Katlian's dark eyes glittered as she frowned, but then she smiled. "Perhaps."

"Do you want me to get her?"

Katlian shook her head. "No, you let her work today. She's going to see Jennifer and I want her to be focused on her work. I will see her later."

Katlian stood up and Derek opened the door for her. She walked out of the clinic, past a few people who were still concerned about the always strong and steadfast Katlian Yazzie breaking down in the waiting room.

Derek ran a hand over his head.

Was this what his rotation with Evelyn Saunders was going to be like? All these relatives coming out of the woodwork and daily emotional reunions? As much as he was all for family coming together, he couldn't let this keep happening.

The office door chimed and a pregnant woman hunched over came in.

"I need help!" she cried out. "I'm in labor and my husband is out in the bush on a logging run."

"Evelyn!" Derek shouted over his shoulder as he dashed toward the woman.

He held on to her as she breathed through a contraction.

"Christina…" Derek said in a soothing tone. "Don't worry we have an OB/GYN here."

Christina nodded. "But it's too soon. Dr. Pearson said last week my baby was breech and he was going to try and turn it this week."

Damn Dr. Pearson.

"He didn't turn it?" Derek asked as he helped Christina toward the exam room while the receptionist worked to rebook the couple of patients who were waiting. She knew the drill when an emergency patient came in.

"He was supposed to turn it today," Christina said. "I was coming here to have it done, but labor started…"

This was why Wolf's Harbor needed a hospital. The air ambulance to take her to Sitka would be ready in thirty minutes, but this baby might be born before they got there.

Evelyn came out of the exam room where she had been going through case files. Her eyes widened as she saw the woman, but it didn't take long before she was helping Derek get the woman up on a stretcher in exam room two, which sometimes acted as an operating room.

"I'm Dr. Saunders and I'm an obstetrician. How far along are you…?"

"Christina," Derek said as he handed Evelyn a box of rubber gloves as if it was second nature.

"Thirty-seven weeks," Christina panted.

"Well, if the baby needs to come anything over thirty-six weeks is safe, Christina. Let's get you draped and then I can see how far along you are."

Derek helped drape Christina while Evelyn helped her remove her clothes.

"Is this your first baby?" Evelyn asked gently.

Christina nodded.

"How far apart are your contractions?"

"Two minutes. They started hard and fast."

She gripped the sides of the gurney and Evelyn reached out and laid her hand on Christina's belly, closing her eyes.

"Derek…" Evelyn said.

"What do you need?" he asked.

Evelyn stood up, pulling off the rubber gloves and dumping them in the waste receptacle. "Can we talk briefly outside?"

"Is everything okay?" Christina asked.

Evelyn smiled. "Perfectly. You're seven centimeters dilated. Still a bit to go, okay? Your water is intact and I'm going to send the nurse in to set up an IV to get some fluids into you and make you more comfortable."

Christina nodded and smiled. "Thank you, Doctor."

Evelyn motioned for them both to leave the exam room. "Can you get Janet in here? Get her to set up an IV and stay with Christina?"

"Sure." Derek went to the front desk and relayed the instructions to Janet, who went straight to work.

Nancy the receptionist had locked the front door and closed the blinds.

"All your patients and Dr. Saunders' patients have been rescheduled," Nancy said. "I'll man the phones. And I'm still trying to get hold of Christina's husband in the logging camp."

"Thanks, Nancy. How about that air ambulance?"

"It'll be ready in thirty minutes, but there's a storm brewing off the coast."

Great.

Derek scrubbed a hand over his face. "Keep them on standby, okay?"

Nancy nodded. "Will do, Dr. Taylor."

Derek turned to Evelyn, who had come out of the exam room.

"Well?" he asked.

"The baby is breech. Frank breech. The baby should've been turned last week."

Derek cursed under his breath. "What do we do?"

Evelyn bit her lip. "Her contractions are strong. Janet is getting a read-out, and it doesn't appear that the baby is in distress. It's just happening so fast."

"So taking them in an air ambulance to Sitka is out of the question?"

"Yeah, that baby is going to move soon, if the contractions and her dilation progress have any say in the matter. As it's a frank breech I may be able to deliver the child vaginally. But it'll be hard and she'll have to work…"

"Your other option?" Although Derek already knew, and it terrified him to the core.

"You have surgical equipment. I've seen it. And I have taken courses in anesthesiology."

"So have I," Derek said. "Do you think it will come to that?"

"I don't know." Evelyn tied her hair back. "Do you have any spare scrubs in the back?"

"Yes. What do you need me to do?"

"Prep surgical supplies, just in case, but I'm hoping that it doesn't result in a crash C-section. Janet has the patient's care in hand. You didn't tell me she was a nurse who had skill in midwifery."

"Well, we never got around to that." Derek took a deep breath. "I'll help any way I can."

Evelyn nodded. "I appreciate it. I've delivered frank breech babies before. It can be done. Protocols have changed. It's not an automatic C-section."

Derek nodded. "I know."

"Good, because it looks like there's going to be a baby born. Today." Evelyn headed off to the storage room to change into scrubs.

He went to collect the surgical supplies, his insides twisting, and tried to shake away all those dark memories that were threatening to bubble up.

There's a supply of blood in the fridge. You're prepared this time.

He had this. This was his patient. He had control. He was prepared for anything.

Vivian's death had taught him to be prepared so more lives could be saved and fewer lives lost. Vivian's death was the reason why he fought so hard for a hospital in Wolf's Harbor. And it wasn't just for crash C-sections, but other traumatic injuries. They needed more room. They needed surgeons here. Qualified people.

But no one ever stayed.

Except him.

And Evelyn?

She could handle it. She was trained for this and he was glad she was here. They were the only hope and he had to pull himself together. There was no time to think about Vivian. Right now he had to help Evelyn save two lives. They needed to be a team and he needed his A-game. Which was exactly what he'd give.

CHAPTER FOUR

DEREK JUMPED INTO the fray and seemed to anticipate her every move. It was nice. It could take time for two doctors to learn each other's cues and timings and work seamlessly together, but with Derek it was as if they had been working together for years.

And that put her at ease about delivering a frank breech baby on her first day back in Wolf's Harbor.

The receptionist, Nancy, helped her into a gown and gloves.

"She's ten centimeters dilated, Dr. Saunders, and her water broke," said Janet. and showed Evelyn the read-out. The baby's heartbeat was strong and everything was going smoothly—except the fact that the baby was heading out upside down. "The contractions are close and strong."

Evelyn nodded. "Thank you, Janet. Christina, I think we're ready to have this baby."

"Tom isn't here," Christina panted. "I can't have this baby without Tom!"

"I don't think the baby is going to wait for Tom," Evelyn said as she took a seat at the end of the bed. She bent down and could see the baby's backside crowning. "In fact I *know* we can't wait for Tom. You're going to have push and push hard, Christina. This baby is breech. But we'll be with you all the way and at the end you'll have your baby, yes?"

Christina nodded, but she was crying.

Derek stepped up and held Christina's shoulders. "I'm here in Tom's place, okay? I'm here for you, and you know I've done this before."

Christina nodded, and Evelyn couldn't help but melt slightly, watching the care and tenderness Derek showed his patient. The gruff exterior was gone and replaced by something tender and compassionate.

It made her heart skip a beat.

She shrugged it off and watched the monitor as another contraction went off. "Come on—now, *push*, Christina. Hard. That's it. Push to ten."

Evelyn kept one eye on the monitors and one eye on the baby. Twenty years ago she'd have been putting Christina under and delivering the baby via C-section, but a frank breech—if the mother and baby were healthy—could be delivered the old-fashioned way. If the baby had been a footling breech it would be a different story.

Still, this was going to be a hard birth.

Janet continued encouraging Christina, and Derek supported their patient as Evelyn guided a beautiful baby girl into the world—bum first.

The baby didn't cry right away, but that wasn't unusual, and Evelyn suctioned the mouth while Janet rubbed the baby vigorously.

There was a fraction of a moment when Evelyn worried, just for a second, that the baby wouldn't cry and she'd have to resuscitate. She shifted her brain to focus on the protocol for that—especially since they weren't in a hospital. But it was only for a fleeting moment, because then the baby took a breath and cried out at the indignity of being cold and pestered.

Evelyn's heart swelled and she smiled behind her surgical mask. This was her favorite part. Life. A healthy baby. She held the little one carefully to get a closer look. Her heart raced as a secret pang of longing coursed through her.

So wonderful. Pure. A new life safely arrived in the world.

The possibilities for this baby were endless. It was thrilling, as always, to be there on day one of a child's life.

"It's a girl!" she announced. "Do you want me to cut the cord?"

Christina nodded. "Tom was going to do it… but, yeah."

Evelyn cut the cord and the placenta was delivered soon after. Janet took the baby to the warmer to rub ointment in her eyes, weigh her and do the heel stick. Everything that needed to be done. But it wasn't long before the baby was brought back to Christina, to be held skin to skin with the relieved mother.

"Excellent work, Dr. Saunders," Derek said as Evelyn finished cleaning up. He was beaming at her. Those intense eyes sparkling with pride. "Seriously—excellent job."

"Thanks to you, as well," she said. "I couldn't have done that without you."

He looked stunned. "I did nothing."

"What do you mean nothing? You have a well-stocked clinic and I didn't have to give you instructions. You knew what to do."

"Still, *you* did all the work," he whispered.

"I don't do much," Evelyn said. "I just catch them."

Derek chuckled and then left the room.

Evelyn passed on the post-op care to Janet. If all went well Christina and the baby could go home today. For a breech birth, it had been almost textbook. And she was relieved that the first birth she'd had to attend to in Wolf's Harbor had been easy.

As she peeled off her gown and gloves Nancy opened the door to the exam room. "Look who I found!" she announced.

A man in flannel and denim, who looked a bit wide-eyed and dazed, stumbled in. "Did I miss it?"

"Tom, I presume?" Evelyn asked with a smile.

"Yeah. I missed it, didn't I?" He rubbed his hand over his head. "I *knew* I shouldn't have gone to work today."

"Everything is fine, Tom. Go meet your daughter."

Tom grinned. "A girl?"

Evelyn watched as Tom went to Christina and bent down to see his newborn daughter. A happy family.

That pang of longing for something she could never have washed over her again.

But you could have it if you want.

She forced that thought away and left the exam room to clean up. The birth had happened so fast. It was only lunch time and they could see their patients in the afternoon. She could still get Jennifer Yazzie in.

Evelyn went to find her file, worried suddenly, because if Dr. Pearson hadn't tried to turn Christina's baby before he left, what was going on with Jennifer and her small measurements?

Nancy was back at the front desk.

"Can you reschedule Jennifer Yazzie for later this afternoon, Nancy?"

"Sure, Dr. Saunders."

Evelyn thanked Nancy and headed to exam room three, which had a desk and was obviously the office for a rotating specialist. It was cramped, and a bit dark, but it worked and that was where she set up her computer.

There weren't many pregnant women in Wolf's Harbor, but there were a couple of six-week check-ups and everyday women's health stuff to deal with. For the most part it was going to be an easy job.

Evelyn fired up her laptop and frowned because the clinic did not appear to have high-speed internet access.

"Have I gone back to the time of dial-up?" she murmured under her breath.

"Yeah, the Wi-Fi here is really not reliable."

Evelyn looked up and saw Derek standing in the doorway. Her cheeks flushed with warmth at being caught muttering to herself.

"It's okay," she said.

"It's just a fact of life at the clinic and in these parts. Life can move a bit slower around here."

"Not for Christina," Evelyn teased. "Thank you again for your help."

Derek nodded. "Like I said, I didn't do anything. You did fantastic, though. You really calmed her down."

"Thanks. Textbook frank breech birth, though. Nothing to it."

She turned back to her computer, embarrassed by the compliment. She knew that she was good—one of the best—but it was always hard for her to take praise when she was just doing her job.

"I was going to head to Sally's next door and grab a quick bite. Do you want to join me?"

The question caught Evelyn off guard. "No, thank you. I want to look up some information, and I have a quick email I want to send to a colleague before I see Jennifer Yazzie this afternoon."

"Anything I can help with?"

"Did the other OB/GYNs confide in you about their patients?"

"No. Not really. They didn't like to talk to a general practitioner who knows nothing."

Evelyn rolled her eyes. "Why does *that* not surprise me?"

Derek shrugged. "You get used to it. Still, it angered me. The people in Wolf's Harbor are my patients long after any temporary specialist is gone." He crossed his arms. "When I came to town fifteen years ago Jennifer was my first patient. She was five years old. I know her medical history pretty well."

"You've been here a long time."

"I like it here. This is home."

"It must be weird, seeing your patients having families of their own. Makes you feel a bit old, doesn't it?"

"Well...*now* it does."

Then Derek smiled, which totally caught her off guard, and she couldn't help but laugh with him.

"So *you're* not opposed to talking over stuff with me?" he asked.

"No. I work better sometimes after talking it out."

"Not surprising. I'm the same. Fire away."

"It's about Jennifer Yazzie."

"What's eating you about Jennifer?"

"I met her when I arrived, and she told me how far along she is, but she's awfully small."

Derek's brow furrowed. "What're you thinking?"

"Anything in her past I should know about? Beyond the obstetrical records?"

"No. She's been healthy. Non-smoker and non-drinker. Are you thinking it's intrauterine growth restriction accounting for her small measurements?"

She was impressed that his mind had immediately gone there.

"I'm hoping it's not, but I'm worried about that. We'd have to get her to Juneau—to a larger hospital to deliver the baby. But I'm hoping she's just carrying small. Some women will do that right until the baby is about to be born. But if not, it could be very dangerous for Jennifer and her baby."

A strange expression crossed Derek's face. "I hope it's not, too. I'm going to grab a bite. You should try and have something to eat."

He left quickly, and Evelyn couldn't help but wonder what had gotten into him. She'd thought he wanted to talk more.

She shrugged it off. She couldn't worry about it right now. She opened Jennifer's file and starting skimming through the various notes made over the course of her pregnancy. Her heart sank as it became apparent that she wasn't the only one who was thinking intrauterine growth restriction.

Damn.

Derek didn't head to Sally's. He didn't feel hungry all of a sudden. Instead he headed down the street to daycare.

It wasn't a bustling daycare center. His daughter was currently the only child in town who needed continuous daycare service during the summer. It was convenient, as she was still a bit sick, and he knew if they'd been in a big city he would have had to arrange for another sitter or taken time off.

Of course if they *had* decided to move to Chicago he would have had his mother there to help—plus most likely he wouldn't have been the only doctor in his practice as he wouldn't have been able to afford to buy a solo practice.

But he loved Wolf's Harbor.

Vivian had been from here, and though she'd had parents elsewhere in Alaska she'd been on her own, and they'd made a vow to raise their children here.

Perhaps if another doctor would come and permanently settle here they could trade off, but that was unlikely.

No one ever stayed.

He opened the door to the daycare center, making the bell jingle as he walked in, and slipped off his shoes. Mo was sitting on the couch. Her round gray-green eyes that were so like his lit up when she saw him. His heart melted. He loved her. She was his world. The only thing besides his practice that kept him going.

"Daddy!"

Derek went over and sat down next to her. "How are you feeling?" he asked.

"Better," Mo chirped.

"Monica's fever has broken this morning,"

said Edna the daycare owner as she came into the room.

"Good."

"You off for the day, Dr. Taylor, or is this just a visit?" Edna asked.

"Just a visit."

Edna smiled and left the room.

Mo curled up next to him, holding her blanket, completely fascinated by the crazy cartoon that was on the television.

Derek ran his hand over her forehead. It was clammy, but no sign of a fever.

"I'm fine, Daddy," Mo said, pushing his hand away, annoyed that he was interrupting her show.

So like Vivian.

Everything about Mo reminded him of his late wife. Her personality. Her attitude. Vivian would have loved everything about Mo, and instead of Edna it would have been Vivian taking care of her.

Edna had been helping him take care of Mo since she was born, and she was a warm, loving caretaker, but it wasn't the same as having a mother. And in that Derek thought he was failing Mo. That he wasn't enough for her.

He sat next to her and mindlessly watched

the cartoon, laughing with her at the parts she thought were funny and wishing he could give her more. But he wasn't sure that he could ever put his heart in jeopardy like that again.

He was frozen.

It had been five years since Vivian died, and he was lonely, but remembering the agony he'd gone through losing her, he knew he could never do that again. Mo didn't remember her mother. Didn't know the pain of losing her. He never wanted to put her through that. He could handle the pain, but he never wanted Mo to feel it.

Mo drifted off to sleep and Derek slid off the couch, helping her lie down and then covering her with the blanket that Vivian had made for her when she was pregnant. The blanket was ratty and worn, but Mo wouldn't be parted with it and Derek wouldn't even try.

Edna came into the room and Derek motioned to her that Mo was sleeping. He waved goodbye to her from the door, put on his shoes and strode out into the drizzly afternoon.

He stopped by Sally's and grabbed a sandwich, and then grabbed one for Evelyn. He didn't know what she'd like, so he stuck with egg salad just in case she was vegetarian.

He'd been impressed with Evelyn's performance in helping Christina and her baby. Maybe if she'd been here when Mo was born Vivian would still be here.

He shook his head, because he couldn't dwell on the what-ifs. Those what-ifs that haunted him nightly.

He rounded the corner to the clinic, and his heart skipped a beat when he saw the town ambulance waiting outside.

He ran into the clinic and saw Nancy looking pale.

"What's going on?" Derek asked.

"Christina started bleeding. Heavily. Dr. Saunders had to transfuse her, but it's not stopping. The air ambulance is waiting to take her to Sitka."

Derek glanced over and saw Tom, looking stunned, holding the baby. He knew that expression all too well.

No. Evelyn has this handled.

They'd been like one being in surgery.

Surgery was not his strong suit. He could get by, but being with Evelyn had made him feel completely at ease. It had been like a beautiful dance, and he couldn't have done it without her.

"Dr. Taylor…?" Tom said.

Derek knelt down in front of Tom. "It'll be okay, Tom. Dr. Saunders is a pro."

There was a commotion from the back and he saw Evelyn helping the paramedics wheel out Christina, who was on oxygen and getting blood.

Derek helped Tom up. "Go with your wife. Take your baby. The nurses in Sitka will help."

"I'm going with Christina, Tom," Janet said as Evelyn and the paramedics loaded Christina into the ambulance.

Derek nodded in acknowledgement and Janet took Tom and led him to the back of the vehicle.

Derek walked back to the exam room where not that long ago they had delivered Christina and Tom's baby. A frank breech that Evelyn had said was "textbook."

He opened the door and saw the blood on the floor. His stomach twisted in a knot—not because of the sight of it, but because all he could see was Vivian on the floor of their home, his arms around her as he tried in futility to help her, begging her to stay with him.

A life was saved today. Two lives.

A sense of pride overcame him.

It was all thanks to Evelyn.

There had been no tragedy here. There could

have been. There might have been. But she had brought hope.

He grabbed a mop, started cleaning up the mess.

Saving lives was all that mattered.

And who will save yours?

CHAPTER FIVE

EVELYN BREATHED A sigh of relief as she watched the air ambulance take off. Christina was stable, and that bleeding might have been the result of anything. It might have been a tear, or a clot, but Evelyn didn't have the means to examine it herself. There was no anesthesiologist on hand. Derek had stocked blood in his clinic, but not enough to do a surgical repair. It was better that the Sitka hospital take care of it. There were more people in Sitka. There were more supplies and specialized instruments that weren't here.

At least Christina was still awake… She must remember to praise Derek later for having that small stock of universal blood on hand. If there hadn't been any it might have been disastrous. Derek's smart thinking in stocking the clinic had probably saved Christina's life.

"Need a lift, Dr. Saunders?"

Evelyn turned to see Joe Yazzie Jr. sitting in the airport.

"I would like that—but I have to confess I left my purse at the clinic."

Joe chuckled. "It's on me. Family and everything."

Evelyn's heart skipped a beat. "I guess you're right. We're cousins, I suppose."

Joe scratched his head. "Yeah, no 'suppose' about it. We are. That's what Léelk'w and my father say. It's nice to meet you, cousin."

Evelyn felt like she'd been sucker-punched. "Did you say Léelk'w? Is she still…?"

Joe beamed. "Alive? Yeah, Léelk'w is still alive and kicking. I don't know if she knows you're back in town. Dad hasn't gotten around to seeing her since he ran into you last night."

There were so many emotions that were swirling around inside Evelyn. Her maternal grandmother was *still alive*? She'd thought she'd died. In fact she'd been led to believe that she'd died. Evelyn had mourned her so long ago, but Léelk'w was still alive.

She felt angry for all the time that had gone by. All the time she'd missed.

And whose fault was that?

She'd written so many letters and never heard back. After a time Evelyn had felt as if Léelk'w must have forgotten her, and as more time went on she assumed that Léelk'w had died.

How had anyone thought that was the best thing for her? How was being separated from you family and not knowing about them *better*? How was Boston better than Wolf's Harbor and not vice versa?

No one had ever taken into account *her* feelings. No one had ever asked her what *she* wanted.

Because you didn't deserve it. Your father didn't get what he wanted so why should you?

She really hated that voice inside her. That internal dialogue that never let her forgive, never let her forget what happened.

"You okay, Dr. Saunders?" Joe Jr. asked.

Evelyn nodded and plastered a brave smile on her face. "Yeah, I'm great—and you know what, Joe? You might as well call me Evelyn. We're cousins, after all."

Joe grinned. "Okay."

Evelyn climbed into his cab and he whisked her back to the clinic.

"Will I see you later with Jennifer?"

"Jennifer couldn't get time off for the afternoon, but we're coming tomorrow first thing."

Evelyn nodded. "Good. I look forward to seeing you both."

Joe parked the cab out front. "We'll see you tomorrow."

She got out and walked back into the clinic. Nancy looked up from the reception desk.

"I tried to get Jennifer Yazzie in…"

"It's okay, Nancy. I spoke with her husband and I know she couldn't get the time off. I'll see her tomorrow."

"I'm headed home. Dr. Taylor hasn't rescheduled his appointments. He said to take the rest of the day off."

Evelyn frowned. "But there's still time left."

"Well, he'll stay here in case there's an emergency, but no regular patients. Do you need me to stay, Dr. Saunders?"

"No, it's fine, Nancy. If Dr. Taylor gave you the rest of the day off, go. It's been one heck of a first day for me, anyways. Thanks for your help."

Nancy smiled. "See you tomorrow, Dr. Saunders."

Evelyn walked back to the exam room, to clean up the mess, and walked in on Derek, mopping the floor. He glanced up as if only just noticing her.

"Need help?" she asked.

"Nope—I got it," he said, not looking up at her. He seemed sad, distant, and she hoped he wasn't mad at her for not cleaning up right away.

"I was coming back to clean." Evelyn grabbed another mop.

"Don't worry about it." Derek sighed. "I've got it mostly cleaned up. But, honestly, a mess like that shouldn't be left."

"And was I supposed to stop trying to save Christina's life and clean the floor?"

Derek rubbed his temple. "No, you're right. Sorry."

"What's wrong?"

"Nothing. Just concerned about my patient."

"She'll be fine. I wanted to congratulate you for having universal blood on hand. That probably saved her life."

"Thanks, but it was you too. Your skills which saved her life."

She helped with the mopping, then glanced up at him. "You're really connected to the people in this town, aren't you?"

He fixed her with a piercing stare—one that made her blood heat with the intensity of it. She was always attracted to stand-offish alpha males, but usually they never wanted anything more to do with her than a quick fling. Just sex. And she could tell this was no exception.

Nathan had wanted more.

The problem was, she hadn't wanted more from Nathan.

Did she want something from Derek? Yeah, she did. It was alarming how much she was attracted to him. How he made her nervous and yet excited. How much he affected her.

No man had ever made her feel this way before, and she wondered if Derek might be the kind of guy who might cure her of her restless nature.

But even if she wished it, it wasn't that way— because she didn't want any of that. It was way too risky.

You're not here to stay. You don't have time for a relationship.

He shrugged. "They're like family, and someone has to be."

She understood that. He was protective of his practice just like her father had been. Where her grandmother had loathed his dedication to Wolf's Harbor, Evelyn had admired him for it.

"Are you okay?" he asked.

"Of course," she said, hoping he didn't detect the nervousness she was feeling.

He cocked his head to the side, as if he didn't quite believe her. As if he knew what she'd been thinking about only moments before.

"It was an intense first day for you," he remarked before going back to his mopping.

Whew.

"Yes," Evelyn replied, relieved.

"It's usually not like this here. It's a quiet town."

"Oh, you *know* that's not a word you should utter after an emergency situation. Especially to a surgeon."

Derek cocked an eyebrow. "Why?"

"'Quiet' means anything but in the emergency room. It'll get busy again now. You just watch."

"I hope you're wrong. We've had enough for one day. Heck, we've had enough for a *month*!"

They laughed together at that.

Just as she had finished disposing of the trash and placing the instruments on a tray to be sterilized she heard the distinct cry of a child in pain.

Derek's head snapped up and he dashed out of the room as if he'd been struck by lightning.

What in the world...?

Evelyn peeled off her rubber gloves and followed him.

An older woman was holding a gauze bandage to a little girl's head, and Evelyn could tell it was soaked through with blood. The girl was clinging to Derek, who was rubbing her back, and as the little girl stopped crying to speak to him she could see brilliant gray-green eyes—*Derek's eyes*—looking up at him.

Now she understood what was keeping him in Wolf's Harbor. It wasn't just his patients who were his family.

He *had* a family. A *real* family.

Great. You're lusting after a married man.

"Is everything okay?" Evelyn asked.

Derek looked at her defeatedly. There was worry etched on his face.

The older woman spoke up, "She was feeling better and running around the house, but then she had a dizzy spell and slipped, hitting her head against a cupboard door. It was a deep gash, so I've brought her here."

"She's my daughter," Derek said. "This is Monica. Mo for short."

She was surprised. Derek didn't wear a wedding ring, and had never mentioned his daughter before, but then again he didn't chat much about his personal life.

She looked at the little girl, bleeding from her head wound, crying and clinging to her father. She had once been that little girl in her father's arms.

Her heart melted. She loved kids.

"Well, why don't you bring her into exam room two and I can look at the gash?" Evelyn suggested gently.

"I can do it," Derek said, not looking at her but holding his daughter close and rubbing her back.

"No, you can't. You're her father. I will do it."

"You're an OB/GYN."

"I'm a surgeon, first and foremost. I think I can suture a wound."

Derek nodded, and then turned to the older woman. "I've got it from here, Edna. Thank you for bringing her in. I'll see you tomorrow."

Edna nodded, but looked worried all the same as she left the clinic.

Derek followed Evelyn into exam room two. His daughter had calmed down and was staring at her, with her head pressed against her father's shoulder. She had the same beautiful eyes and tawny skin, and the most beautiful curly sandy-colored hair that Evelyn had ever seen.

Derek set her down on the paper-covered exam table and Monica still watched her.

"Who's that, Daddy?" she asked.

"I'm Dr. Evelyn Saunders, but you can call me Evie."

Monica smiled. "I'm Monica, but you can call me Mo."

Evelyn smiled at her. "Well, Mo, can I take a look at your head?"

Mo looked at her father, unsure.

"It's okay. Dr. Saunders is nice."

"Evie, Daddy," Mo corrected.

"Oh, I don't let *him* call me Evie. He's too grumpy," Evelyn teased, and Mo's eyes twinkled and she laughed.

Derek smiled tenderly at his daughter, but didn't look at her.

"How old are you, Mo?" Evelyn asked.

"Five—well, I just turned five."

"It was your birthday recently?"

"In March," Derek said. "Not *that* recent."

"I wasn't talking to you," Evelyn teased.

Mo laughed, and then winced.

"Can I look at your head?"

Mo still looked uncertain, but Derek gently prompted her and Evelyn was able to remove the gauze from her head.

"Ouch—you're being super-brave, Mo."

Evelyn brought over a suture kit and Mo eyed it with worry.

"What's that?" she asked.

"This is going to fix that nasty cut on your head and make you feel a lot better." Evelyn got some numbing agent out. "In fact, looking at it, I don't even think I'll have to stitch that. I think we can get away with cleaning and some paper sutures—which is a fancy word for a plaster."

"Really?" Mo asked.

Evelyn nodded. "Yep."

"Edna said I would have to get stitches cause it bled so much. I got blood on my blankie." Mo held up a ratty old crocheted afghan.

"Who made that for you?" Evelyn asked.

"My mommy."

"I'm sure your mommy can clean it for you."

"Mommy is dead."

She saw Derek stiffen and she looked up at him quickly. Now she understood. All the pain in his eyes was the same pain that she'd seen in her father's.

Evelyn's heart melted even more. Sure, Derek was sexy, and she was highly attracted to him physically, but this was something more. This was something far more dangerous. She felt sorry for him handling this alone.

She remembered all those times she'd snuck downstairs and caught her father crying, mourning her mother. She knew the keen sense of loneliness he'd felt.

"I'm sorry to hear that," Evelyn said gently. "How about your daddy? He can clean it for you, right?"

Mo nodded. "He can."

"That's good. He'll get it all cleaned up and you'll forget that this even happened." Evelyn pulled out the antibacterial cleaner and some gauze.

"Will this hurt?" Mo asked.

"Truth?"

Mo nodded.

"A little bit," Evelyn said. "But if we get this cleaned out and fixed up then it won't hurt later and it will heal right up. Kids have an amazing super-power."

"Oh?"

"They heal super-fast." Evelyn smiled. "If *I'd*

cut my head that bad I would probably need stitches, and it wouldn't heal as fast as your cut will heal. Plus, I think this would be an awesome opportunity to get some ice cream out of your dad."

Mo's eyes lit up. "Okay!"

"Thanks." Derek chuckled.

Evelyn grinned. "Can you lie back for me? I'll get that cleaned out. It's going to sting a little bit, but it'll be over with soon—I promise."

Mo lay down and closed her eyes as Evelyn began.

"Why did it bleed so much, Evie?" Mo asked.

"Your head always bleeds a lot because there are tons of blood vessels in your scalp that are close to the surface—so when you get a cut it bleeds a lot."

Evelyn finished cleaning the wound and then placed Steri-strips over the wound and a bandage.

"There—all done, and you were incredibly brave."

Evelyn helped her sit up. Mo's little hand slipped into hers, and in the little girl so attached to her father Evelyn saw herself.

She had once been Mo.

The only difference was that she'd remembered

bits and pieces about her mother, and she'd had her mother's extended family reminding her of who her mother was.

"You can take her home now," Evelyn said to Derek. "You know the drill. I can manage closing up the clinic."

"Thank you, Evelyn." Derek scooped up his daughter, but didn't look at her.

"Thanks, Evie," Mo chirped. "Daddy, can Evie come over for dinner? Evie, do you want to come over for dinner?"

Evelyn was taken aback by the sweet, heartfelt invitation. But Derek's eyes were wide as he tried to come up with an excuse and she knew that she couldn't intrude on their dinner. Derek was clearly uncomfortable, and now she understood. He had a daughter to protect.

Evelyn wasn't going to be here in Wolf's Harbor permanently, and Mo had lost her mother. The last thing Mo needed was some strange woman coming over to the house and getting attached. Evelyn didn't want things to be harder on Mo. She knew personally how that could feel, and she didn't want this poor little girl to have any more trauma.

It wouldn't be fair.

"That's very sweet of you to invite me, Mo," Evelyn started. "Maybe another night?"

Mo looked sad, and Derek looked at her. "Tonight is fine, Evelyn—if you're available. Mo is right. You *should* come over for dinner. It's the least we can do to say thank you for helping us."

Mo looked so hopeful that Evelyn didn't want to disappoint her. And she didn't really have any other plans, except continuing to clean that atrocious apartment.

Make an excuse. Don't go.

Only Evelyn couldn't break that sweet little girl's heart. She knew what that girl was feeling deep down. She felt a connection to her.

"Sure. I can come for dinner."

"Great!" Mo beamed.

"Will Joe Jr. know where you live?" Evelyn asked, her stomach swirling as every fiber of her being told her she was foolish for agreeing to have dinner with a widower and his daughter.

Derek nodded. "Yes, he'll know. We'll see you at seven?"

"Bye, Evie!" Mo chirped happily as Derek walked out of the exam room with his daughter in his arms.

Evelyn let out a breath she hadn't known she

was holding as she tried to figure out a way to get out of it without hurting Mo's feelings, but the more she thought about it the more she realized she was stuck.

What harm can come from one little dinner?

She sighed, thinking those were famous last words—because she knew exactly what the harm could be. How it could tear someone's heart apart.

She needed to find a way out of this. Not only for her sake, but for little Mo's heart too.

CHAPTER SIX

WHAT DO YOU bring to dinner with a man who probably hates you and his cute five-year-old daughter? That was the crux of the matter.

And *that* was an overreaction. Derek didn't hate her. He didn't know her. He tolerated her, and that was something different.

She couldn't blame him for being a bit cool.

She *got* why he was defensive about his practice—especially in light of Dr. Pearson messing up earlier. It was hard trying to protect your patients and raise a child on your own. She'd seen her father struggle. And if she was in the same position she would be untrusting of temporary doctors creating more work for her or jeopardizing her patients.

So, she was not really looking forward to this dinner, but she'd put on her best face and get through it.

And if there was one thing her grandmother had taught her about attending dinner parties it was that you didn't go empty-handed, but Evelyn had no idea what to bring. She finally settled on a bottle of wine that she'd found in the apartment and then went next door to Sally's before the bakery closed and bought the cupcakes that Sally told her Mo particularly liked.

Joe Jr. picked her up in the cab.

"Hey, Evie, I was surprised to get your call."

Evelyn slid in beside him. "Why is that?'

Joe shrugged. "The other doctors never went out. Never really socialized. Well, except Dr. Pearson—but he had his own car and usually he went to Hoonah or a bigger community to socialize."

"I guess I'm the exception."

"Where are you headed?" Joe asked.

"Dr. Taylor's place. He said you would know the directions."

"I sure do," Joe said, nodding. "It's just outside of town."

"Great."

Joe headed down the main street and they chatted easily about things, but when they turned off the main road toward a gravel road that wound its way through the forest Evelyn's pulse kicked up a notch.

The trees were denser, but she recognized each curve and bend in the road.

It can't be.

Her stomach flip-flopped and then bottomed out when Joe pulled up at the end of the road and she found herself staring at the little log house that was set in the forest near the water.

She *knew* this road.

She'd memorized it in her dreams, though as the years had gone on it had faded, but now, as she gazed at the little cabin, she knew without a doubt where she was.

The place she'd dreamed about. The place she'd longed for. One of the last places she'd truly been happy because her father had been alive and they had been happy together.

Home.

Except it wasn't home. Not *her* home. Not anymore.

"Here we are!" Joe said.

"Thanks, Joe." Evelyn paid him and then slipped out of the taxi. She waved as Joe drove away and then just stood in front of the place she'd once called home. If she closed her eyes she could almost see herself running from the front door and down toward the water to greet her father.

She could still smell the scent of pine in the wood stove on those cold winter nights.

And she could remember how empty the house had felt when she'd realized that her father was never coming home.

The door opened and Derek stepped out.

"Evelyn? Have you been standing out here long?"

"Not long." Evelyn smiled and held out the box of cupcakes. "For Mo. How is she feeling?"

"She's asleep," Derek said, taking the cupcakes.

"Do you want me to come back? I can call Joe…" In fact she was slightly relieved that maybe she'd be able to get out of this dinner and she wouldn't have to spend any time in this house.

"No, come in."

"I'm not sure I can," she said.

"Why?" Derek asked, confused. "Is it because of me?"

"No."

He cocked an eyebrow. "Then what is it? It was Mo's invitation, wasn't it? It freaked you out. Look, it shocked me too. She's never really taken to someone like that before."

"It's not Mo's invitation. It's complicated."

A warm smile tugged at his lips and it sent a zing of electricity through her. His smile made her weak in the knees, and he was so much more tempting when that smile was directed at her. It was a potent smile.

"Complicated I get," he said gently.

Evelyn chuckled and tucked her hair behind her ear in a nervous twitch. "I just didn't expect… I didn't expect you to live *here*."

Derek turned and looked back at his house. "Something wrong with my house?"

Evelyn bit her lip and then sighed. "I used to live here, Derek. This used to be my home before I was taken away."

There were a lot of excuses that Derek had been expecting to hear from her.

Before Vivian, women had come on to him all the time, even if he hadn't been interested in them, but they'd soon lost interest in him when he'd told them his plans to move to Alaska.

He tried once to date, a couple of years after Vivian had died, but the woman had learned he had a daughter, emotional baggage in the form of a deceased wife, and a practice that took up a lot of his time. It had been enough to scare her away and had soured him on dating anyone.

Which had always been fine with him. Until now.

He'd seen the look of shock in Evelyn's eyes when he'd explained that Mo was his daughter and that he was a widower. He'd seen that pity and he didn't want it. Not from her.

He wanted something completely different from her. Derek didn't want Evelyn just to see him as a single dad and a widower. He enjoyed working with her. It felt natural and she kept him focused. She chased away the nightmares. The numbness. He wanted her to see him as just himself.

Who he really was.

And who is that?

He wasn't sure he knew anymore.

All he knew was that look of pity with the head-tilt, and he didn't want to see it from her.

He'd honestly been expecting her to call and cancel the dinner, even though such a call would have absolutely devastated Mo. So he was happy she was here, because of Mo's feelings, but when she hadn't come in right away he'd been pretty sure she was going to bolt.

He hadn't been expecting her to say that his home had once been hers. And he'd had no idea that he was living in Dr. Thorne Saunders' home. Evelyn's childhood home. He'd bought it from a logger who'd worked here in Wolf's Harbor for a few summers and then decided to join a crab fishing boat. He'd sold the home to Derek when he'd first arrived and then Vivian had moved in.

He knew about Evelyn's past—sort of. Different people had told him about her parents dying and her having to leave Wolf's Harbor, but that was it.

People didn't talk about Thorne Saunders besides saying he'd been an excellent doctor. And no one had told him this was Thorne's former home. The name on the deed before the man he'd bought this house from was L. Yazzie, and he'd assumed it had belonged to the Yazzie family at one point. He hadn't known the connection between the Yazzies and Thorne until recently.

Now it made perfect sense. He just hadn't seen it before, even though Evelyn had had that emotional reunion with Joe Yazzie when she'd first arrived.

He could only imagine what she was going through, but though he knew he should tell her it would be OK to leave or call Joe to come get her, he didn't want her leaving.

He was lonely, and Evelyn was someone bright, vibrant. Someone who excited him. And he wanted her to stay. He wanted to talk to an adult. To have a conversation and enjoy a glass of wine.

"Come inside," he said, surprising himself.

This was not treating Evelyn like all the other doctors who'd come through town. He'd never invited *them* over. They'd never known he had a daughter.

Yeah, but none of them had really cared about this place beyond serving their time.

Evelyn came from Wolf's Harbor. She had an emotional investment in the people. She cared. And it was nice to have that in common with another physician in town.

Derek wanted her to stay, even if he knew it would be hard for her *and* for him. He liked working with her. He liked talking with her about medicine. He was lonely for that.

Evelyn coming here was like a breath of fresh air—one he didn't want to end.

He'd felt as if he was suffocating before.

Evelyn nodded and he gently placed his hand on the small of her back to guide her in. Just that simple touch did something to him. It sent a zing of anticipation, of electricity through him and he was taken aback by it.

It made him think things that weren't chaste.

Don't think of her like that.

Only around her, it seemed, he couldn't help himself, and constantly thought about her *like that*. He thought about what it would be like to run his hands through her hair, to taste her lips and feel her body flush against his.

You're treading on dangerous ground.

Derek snatched his hand back as quickly as he'd placed it there. Then shut the door as Evelyn stood in the foyer and stared up at the exposed beams.

"Wow, it's brighter in here. I don't remember the exposed beams."

"Yeah, I did some renovations when I first bought the place. It was a bit dark…" He closed his eyes, cursing himself inwardly. Maybe her father had built this home and he was insulting it.

Evelyn smiled at him and unwound the scarf she was wearing to hang it up on the hook by the door. "Yes, it was. It was cozy, but I like the exposed beams and the skylights. That's a nice touch."

"Thanks. The kitchen is in the back still." Derek started walking toward the kitchen that he'd updated as well.

Evelyn followed him silently and it was awkward. You could cut the tension with a knife.

Why couldn't this be easier?

You know why. It's because you find her attractive and you hate yourself just a little right now.

There was no time for him to think of his selfish wants or desires. He was a dad first and a doctor second. That was all.

He didn't deserve anything else.

He couldn't get involved with someone who would leave town in a couple of months, and he certainly didn't want Mo to get attached to someone who was leaving soon.

He set the box of cupcakes down on the counter and ran a hand over his head, unsure of what to do. It had been long time since he'd been on a date.

This is not a date. It's a dinner for a colleague. It's a thank-you dinner.

"Is everything okay with you?" Evelyn asked, standing in the kitchen door.

"Yeah. I… I didn't think that you would come," he admitted.

Evelyn chuckled. "Truth?"

"Yeah."

"I almost didn't," she said.

He smiled and then they both laughed nervously, the tension melting away.

"I will say it's not because of Mo. That's not the reason why I almost didn't come."

"Then what is it?" he asked, shocked but secretly pleased. Usually it was his status as a single dad that threw women off.

"You haven't exactly been friendly or welcoming to me since I arrived. Though if you had to deal with Dr. Pearson for the last month I can understand a fraction of that and I don't even know the man."

"Ah, yes. I have to apologize about that."

She cocked an eyebrow. "Really?"

He nodded. "I have control issues when it comes to my clinic."

She laughed gently. She had a beautiful smile. "I hadn't noticed."

"I care a lot about my patients."

"I have noticed that, and I admire it."

His pulse kicked up a notch at the compliment.

"You do? Most people…they don't understand that."

"I do."

"I know. It's refreshing."

"How so?" she asked.

"Most doctors who come through here don't care. They do their time, don't interact and move on. You seem to care. You put yourself out there to get to know your patients."

"I love my job, and an important part of the job is trust. I give it my all. And Wolf's Harbor was my home once. My father loved his patients too. Coming here is a way to honor him." She looked away, pink coloring her cheeks, as if she was afraid of him seeing her get emotional.

It touched him. Deeply.

There was much to admire about Evelyn Saunders.

Dammit. It was going to be hard to treat her like all the others who'd come before her.

"Well, I'm truly sorry if I've been cold to you. Thank you for coming here and making Mo's night—despite the fact you think I'm an intolerable grump."

"You're welcome."

"Would you like a glass of wine?" he asked.

"Sure."

"Take a seat in the living room and I'll bring it out."

Evelyn nodded and headed to the living room while Derek pulled down two wineglasses from a cupboard. He opened the red wine she'd brought and poured two glasses. He looked at the label and was surprised she'd been able to get such an expensive bottle of wine in Wolf's Harbor.

He picked up the glasses and set them on a tray that also held some cheese and crackers.

Evelyn was sitting on the large sectional couch that was set in front of the fire that he'd started. She was staring up at the wooden beams in awe. Or at least he hoped it was awe and not something like boredom.

He thought again how it really had been a while since he was on a date.

This isn't a date. Remember that.

He cringed inwardly. This wasn't a date. He was *not* on a date.

"This still looks the same," she remarked. "I'm glad you kept this the same."

"I didn't really change this room. I liked it cozy," he said as he set the tray on the coffee table and then handed her a glass.

"Wow," she said.

"What?" he asked, sitting down next to her.

"You are so neat and organized. Your house is immaculate. Very smooth compared to what Dr. Pearson left me."

He breathed a sigh of relief and chuckled.

"Well, my mom has a very successful catering company in Chicago so I grew up learning how to entertain, I suppose. I was a waiter for many years when I was working my way through college. As for the cleanliness—that's thanks to a cleaning lady and the fact that Mo and I don't spend much time here. I'm sure if I were a stay-at-home dad this place would be a lot more disorganized."

"Order is something you can control."

He cocked an eyebrow. "What do you mean?"

"The clinic is immaculate too. You like to be able to control things, and when things are out of your hands you don't like it. I get it. I respect it. Because I'm the same way."

"I'm glad," Derek said quietly, and they sat in silence, listening to the fire crackle and trying to ignore the awkward silence between them.

"Thanks for your help today and for cleaning up the mess I left," she said.

"It's okay. It's just…it was intense today, but you were there for Christina and you were amazing."

"Yeah, she's stable now, and they fixed the tear in her uterine wall. She had a fibroid, and with the force of her labor and a frank breech birth it tore. I didn't know she had fibroids. Of course, she was supposed to have the baby turned by Dr. Pearson and that never happened."

"Yeah, well, I'm not too impressed with him."

"There's something else." Evelyn set her wineglass down on the table. "Jennifer Yazzie's measurements have been small."

"Are you still concerned about intrauterine growth restriction?"

"Yeah." She sighed sadly.

"I'm sorry. I don't know a lot about that. You don't encounter it much up here."

"It's okay. It's just that you seemed bothered by it before when I brought it up," she said.

"Well, I worry about… My wife died here after giving birth to Mo. If she'd been in a city she would've survived."

"I'm sorry."

And she reached out to touch him, placing her delicate hand on his thigh. There was no pity in her beautiful deep brown eyes. Just heartfelt sympathy.

He shrugged, but said nothing else. It still ate at him. He should've got Vivian to a hospital, but her pregnancy had been textbook and she'd wanted a home birth.

It's your fault. You should've convinced her to go to Juneau.

"So is there anything else?" he asked, ignoring that voice in his head—the voice that kept him up at night, reminding him how he'd failed Vivian.

"Well, I see that Dr. Pearson suspected intra-uterine growth restriction, but I don't think he told her."

"No, he probably didn't." Derek rolled his eyes.

"Well, I'm going to speak to the medical board, because that's two patients here that were not dealt with properly. What else has been missed?"

"He was here for three months, but Jennifer is getting close to term now, so how many other people didn't see it. Now you understand why I'm mad that I'm the only one who stays. This constant rotation of doctors is not good for the people here. Sometimes it does more harm than good. And we need a hospital. Even if it's small. We need a hospital with regular staff so that when situations like what happened to Christina or Mo arise then they can be taken care of right away. I've been fighting for years to make it happen, but money is tight."

She nodded. "A hospital would be great, but it wouldn't have saved my father's life."

"What happened to your father?" he asked. "I know that he passed, but no one has told me how."

"He was walking through town to..." She trailed off. "To visit someone and it was foggy. A logging truck that was speeding came through the fog and my father was hit. He was killed instantly. There was nothing to be done. Even if there had been a hospital the damage was too great. No doctor could've saved him."

Derek could see the hint of tears in her eyes, but there was something else there. Something she was not telling him. Just as he wasn't telling *her* the whole truth. How he'd redone the kitchen because that was where Vivian had died and he didn't want to see the wooden floors that were stained after her death. He wanted no part of that room to remind him that she'd collapsed there. That she'd died there.

"I'm sorry, Evelyn. I'm sorry that happened to you."

She smiled. "I'm sorry about your wife. And I'm sorry that I'm only here for a short time, just like everyone else."

Their gazes locked and in her eyes he could see pain just like his pain, reflected back at him. They had so much in common when it came to that, but he also felt something else and his pulse kicked up a notch.

His gaze turned to her pink full lips, the flood of color that was in her smooth tan cheeks and her long slender neck. He had the urge to reach out and touch her. To kiss those lips and feel the silkiness of her long red hair.

It shocked him, but also thrilled him that he was feeling this way.

Get a hold of yourself.

"I'm glad you were there today." He looked away. "For both Christina and Mo."

"Thank you. I'm glad I was there too." She looked down at her empty wineglass.

Tension hung in the air, electric and crackling. How long had it been since he'd felt this way? It had been too long. He'd forgotten what it was like. He'd forgotten what it was like to feel so alive.

He looked back at her. "I'm sorry I get so possessive over my patients and my home. Even though I wasn't born here, Wolf's Harbor *is* my home."

"I understand," she whispered. "That this is your home."

"Isn't this *your* home?" he asked.

"No," she whispered. "It hasn't been my home for some time."

He wanted to tell her it could be. Because they needed her medical skill.

He didn't want her to stay for any other reason. *Liar.*

He had to put some physical distance between them before he did something he would regret.

Would you regret it?

"Would you like another…?" He leaned forward, but he was gripping the glass too tight and it shattered and cut his hand. "Dammit!"

He got up and ran to the kitchen to inspect the damage.

Evelyn followed him. "Let me see."

"It's fine. It's small and superficial."

"Let me see," she repeated, taking his hand.

Her touch sent a shiver through him. Her skin was soft, but her grip firm. A surgeon's hand. Delicate, long fingers. They were hands that had been taken care of.

"See," he murmured. "Superficial."

"Not even a shard of glass in there."

She looked up at him. They were close and he could see how long her lashes really were.

Evelyn cleared her throat. "Do you have a first aid kit?"

"Yeah, in the powder room over there—under the sink."

She disappeared and Derek took a deep breath. He had to get control. He was made of stronger stuff than this.

She returned with the kit and opened it, pulling out gauze and ointment. She bent over his hand and went to work. He could smell the scent of her shampoo. It was coconut. It reminded him of summer. Hot summers with his friends on the beaches of Lake Michigan, swimming and trying not to get too burnt.

"There," she said, wrapping his hand because the cut was on his palm. "You had some Steri-strips, so I put a couple on just to make it easier on you."

"Thank you," he said, his voice hitching.

Their eyes locked and they didn't say anything. Against every rational thought in his head he reached out and touched her cheek. She sighed when he touched her, closing her eyes, and he bent down, his lips barely grazing hers. His pulse thundered between his ears…

"Daddy?"

Evelyn jumped back, as did Derek when he heard Mo call from the other room.

She came into the kitchen. "Evie! You came!"

Evelyn smiled and cleared her throat nervously. "You bet I did. A promise is a promise."

Mo looked at his hand. "What happened, Daddy?"

"I cut it. Just an accident. Dr. Saunders fixed it for me."

Mo beamed. "Good job, Evie."

Evelyn picked up the box of cupcakes. "I brought you these from Sally's. How's your head?"

"Ooh, yum! My head hurts a little. Do you want to come see my room?"

Evelyn looked at him, as if asking for permission. He appreciated that. He nodded. "Go ahead."

"Sure," Evelyn said.

Mo took her hand and led her out of the kitchen while Derek tried to regain some of his composure.

It had just been a light kiss, barely a kiss, but it had seared his soul. Then Mo had almost walked in on them, and that was a scary thought indeed.

He couldn't let that happen again.

Even if he wanted it to happen again.

Badly.

CHAPTER SEVEN

EVELYN DID NOT sleep a wink that night.

The rest of the evening had been completely awkward, but little Mo hadn't seemed to notice at all. She'd been happy as a lark as they'd had a dinner of macaroni and cheese with a side of chicken fingers.

Derek had barely looked at her, and when he had talked to her he'd referred to her as "Dr. Saunders." Still, there had been some stolen, heated glances which had made her pulse quicken, her blood burn and her guilt to go into overdrive.

Mo had almost caught them kissing.

She didn't even want to *think* of what it would have done to Mo if she'd seen them. She remembered when she'd walked in on her father kissing Jocelyn and how it had made her feel to see her father with someone who was not her mother.

Evelyn didn't want Mo to go through that confusion. Or feel guilty later for destroying her father's happiness. She would never forgive herself for ruining her father's happily-ever-after.

As much as she had wanted that kiss to continue, it was good that it had been interrupted. It was good that it hadn't continued for Mo's sake.

And she did really like Mo.

Mo was the sweetest, most darling girl Evelyn had ever met. When she pictured having a daughter, someone like Mo was what she pictured.

But being with Mo just reminded her of what she would never have. Of course she didn't deserve to have it.

Finally her alarm went off and she rolled over and shut it off, groaning because she'd spent the night tossing and turning.

She just hoped Derek and their almost kiss didn't make things awkward.

Evelyn dragged herself out of bed. She got ready as quickly as she could and saw that it was still early. She could probably beat Derek into the office and then lock herself away in an exam room until Jennifer came.

Even though it meant that she would have to drink the horrible instant coffee that had been left in the apartment because she hadn't had a chance to go shopping yet.

It would be worth it.

She didn't want to run into Derek at Sally's and have some weird, tension-filled meet-up that Sally would be privy to and that would soon become the talk of the town. She might have been away for a long time, but she still knew how these towns worked.

As she rounded the corner she ran smack-dab into something hard and warm.

Arms came around her to steady her. "Hey, watch out... Evelyn."

Evelyn winced and looked up to see that Derek was the warm, hard wall she'd managed to run into.

"Derek," she said uneasily. "I was about to start my day. How's your hand?"

She knew she was babbling, but it couldn't be helped. This was exactly what she'd wanted to avoid. It didn't have to be awkward. They were professionals.

"Me too—and good," he responded, slightly stunned.

"You were trying to avoid me, weren't you?" she teased. "Just like I was trying to avoid you. Unsuccessfully, I might add, as we're in such a small town."

"Yeah…" He chuckled and rubbed a hand over his head. "I suppose I was."

"Look, what almost happened was a mistake. It doesn't have to happen again. It *won't* happen again."

He nodded. "It's not that I… I have Mo to think about. But I want you to know that I don't regret what almost happened. Just that with Mo I have to be careful."

"I know. I agree. I wouldn't want her to get hurt. I just want us to work together without it being weird."

Derek sighed. "Me too."

"Good. I'll see you in there, then?"

"Yeah." He started to walk back to Sally's and then stopped. "Look, don't drink that horrible stuff from the apartment. I'll get you a coffee."

"You don't have to do that," she said. Even though she was secretly pleased that he was offering to buy her a coffee. It was a sweet thing to do. What colleagues did.

"Hey, it's what coworkers do. You can get the next round." He turned back around and then headed down the alley toward Sally's.

Evelyn breathed a sigh of relief. She was glad they were going to try and work together, but there was a part of her that was kind of sad that that was all it could ever be.

Why do you want more? You never want more.

Which was true.

She never wanted more out of a relationship. Her relationships never lasted because she wasn't sure that she ever wanted to settle down or have kids. She loved kids, but she knew what it was like to lose both parents. To be taken away from everyone and everything you'd ever known and be sent to the other side of the country.

She knew that pain and she was sure that she never wanted to put a child through that—because there were no guarantees in life and that wasn't a risk she was willing to take.

It was better this way, and she was glad that Derek was on board with it. That they could be professional about their almost-kiss.

The non-kiss.

Just thinking about the almost-kiss caused her heart to kick up a notch, her blood to heat and her body to react as she thought about his arms around her. His lips brushing over hers. All she could think about was him, and she couldn't remember the last time a man had made her feel this way.

Certainly not Nathan.

There had been an attraction with Nathan, but nothing like this mooning, consuming desire that she seemed to be having for Derek.

Get a grip, Evelyn. Seriously.

This was going to be a long, long day if she didn't get her mind off Derek and focused on something else. Anything else.

She unlocked the clinic and flicked on the lights, setting her travel coffee mug on the counter in order to pick up the first file in the small stack that was waiting for her.

Jennifer Yazzie was coming in for the first appointment today, after having to miss yesterday's due to the excitement Christina had caused.

The bell over the door jingled and Janet came in.

"Good morning, Dr. Saunders."

"Good morning, Janet. When did your flight get in from Sitka?"

"Late last night."

"Shouldn't you be home, resting?" Evelyn asked. "I can't begrudge you that after your amazing work with Christina yesterday and flying to Sitka."

Janet beamed. "Thank you, Dr. Saunders, but

I'm fine really. It's only an hour flight, gate to gate, and I'm a bit of a night hawk anyways."

Evelyn grinned. "How *is* Christina?"

"Stable when I left her last night. They named the baby Evie, by the way. Not Evelyn, but Evie. Close to your name."

She blushed and felt very honored. "That's very sweet of them, but Christina did all the work."

Janet handed her an envelope. "Her post-op notes and information from the surgeon in Sitka for Christina's file. Do you need anything particular prepped for this morning, Dr. Saunders?"

"The ultrasound would be great. I'm having Jennifer Yazzie in and I want to check her measurements."

Janet nodded. "Of course, Dr. Saunders. I'll prime the machine now."

Evelyn turned back to Jennifer's chart, reading over all the notes and information about her pregnancy. She wanted to formulate a plan now, since Jennifer was so far along. She didn't want this baby or Jennifer to die because of lack of healthcare.

Besides, Jennifer was sort of family, even though Evelyn didn't know her particularly well. She would hate for something to happen to the next generation of Yazzies. She wasn't going to lose anyone on her watch during her stay in Wolf's Harbor. She was here to save lives, just like her father had.

She smiled to herself, and when the bell jingled at the front door she didn't look up. It was probably Derek with the coffee.

"I hope you didn't let Sally overload it with sugar. Yesterday she added so much to my coffee my back teeth got a sugar rush."

"I don't have coffee," a frail voice responded, barely a whisper.

The hair on the back of Evelyn's neck stood on end and her hand shook as she turned around slowly.

The woman before her was someone she'd thought she'd never see again. She had osteoporosis, and the once-ebony hair was white, with a few strands of black woven through. Her face was wrinkled, and she still wore the traditional abalone earrings that had always fascinated her as a child when she was in her arms.

And although she tried to hold back the rush of emotion she just couldn't.

"Léelk'w…" Evelyn whispered, tears stinging her eyes.

Léelk'w smiled at her brightly. "You *do* remember me, then?"

Evelyn laughed and ran into her arms.

Léelk'w whispered words in her mother's language but Evelyn couldn't find the words to speak back. It was too hard.

"You must speak English first here, Evelyn. No one knows Tlingit."

Evelyn sighed and stared up at her grandmother, annoyed that another note had been sent home from the principal about her using what he assumed were curse words in another language directed to other kids.

"I'll try, Grandma. I'm just so used to speaking—"

Her grandmother cut her off. "You're doing it again. English, please."

Evelyn began to cry. Tears rolled down her cheek.

"Ladies don't cry, Evelyn. You are a Saunders woman and we are strong. Resilient. Never show your tears."

"Yes. I'll try to fit in better, Grandma."

Her grandmother smiled. "I know you will."

She swallowed down the tears, hearing her grandmother's words in her head.

Evelyn broke the connection and took a step back. "Joe Jr. told me that you were still in town."

Léelk'w cocked an eyebrow. "You mean he told you that I was still *alive*. You're just putting it nicely."

Evelyn chuckled. "I suppose so."

She wanted to ask why Léelk'w had never written to her, never called, but she was too afraid. Too afraid of being hurt. Because she really hadn't fitted into Boston well and maybe she'd never really fitted in to Wolf's Harbor either.

You need to know.

"Why didn't you write or call?" Evelyn asked.

Léelk'w was stunned. "Your grandmother had a private number that was blocked. I wrote, but all my letters were returned to sender."

It should have shocked Evelyn, but it didn't. It sounded exactly like her grandmother.

Which made her angry.

"Are you okay, Evie?" Léelk'w asked.

"I'm fine. I'm glad to see that you're still here."

Léelk'w grinned. "I'm in my nineties. My life expectancy is not the best."

Evelyn frowned. "Are you ill? Is that why you're here?"

"No, I came to talk to you about Jennifer."

"I can't do that. It's doctor-patient confidentiality."

Léelk'w snorted. "We're family."

"Well, yes…sort of." She instantly regretted the words as she said them.

Great way of mending fences, Evelyn.

Léelk'w didn't look fazed. "I *knew* that your father's mother would try to erase all you'd learned up here. I knew that she would turn you into the kind of person your father was when he first arrived in Wolf's Harbor."

Evelyn sighed and walked back to her pile of charts. "It has nothing to do with my late grandmother."

"I hadn't heard that she'd passed. I'm sorry."

There was genuine regret there. Evelyn nodded, but couldn't look Léelk'w in the eye. "It's regulations. I'm bound by certain laws, and discussing Jennifer's file without her presence is against them."

Léelk'w crossed her arms. "I can wait until Jennifer comes. She wants me there when the baby is born. Just like I was there when your mother had you. We're blood."

Evelyn's stomach twisted in a knot. They might be related by DNA, but she wasn't sure that they were family. Not anymore. It was her fault that her father had died and she'd been was sent away.

They'd been estranged for so long.

She wasn't sure she could ever go back.

You're scared to try.

"That's fine." Evelyn turned back to her work and tried not to think about her mother or about her childhood.

If she hadn't agreed to take over Stefanie's practice she wouldn't be here in Wolf's Harbor. She'd thought that while she was here she might be able to lay some ghosts to rest, but she was finding it particularly difficult to do that.

It seemed that the ghosts of her past didn't want to be laid to rest. They seemed to pop up unexpectedly and at the most inconvenient times.

"You have closed your heart," Léelk'w said out loud.

"What?" Evelyn asked, stunned.

Léelk'w sighed. "I can't fault you for that. You never got to grieve for your father and I don't think you forgave him for almost marrying Jocelyn."

That struck a chord, but she was about to make her excuses, because she didn't want to talk about Jocelyn. If Jocelyn hadn't existed then her father would never have gone out that night to visit her. But she'd ruined Jocelyn's life, and there was no way Evelyn could make it up to her.

Maybe if you did you wouldn't be so afraid of settling down and having a family.

She was going to say something to respond to that, but the door chimed and Derek walked in, carrying two coffees.

"Dr. Taylor," Léelk'w said stiffly which caused Evelyn to raise an eyebrow in question.

"Katlian, good to see you."

"Liar," Léelk'w muttered, but there was a twinkle in the old woman's eyes.

Evelyn shook her head and Derek set a coffee in front of her. "For you."

"Thanks. I appreciate it."

"I felt bad that you were avoiding Sally's because of possibly running into me," he said.

Evelyn was going to respond, but she saw that Léelk'w was craning her neck, trying to listen. And she couldn't help but laugh.

"Thanks," Evelyn said. "I was just in a rush. I wanted to look over my charts for the day. Janet is back as well."

Derek nodded, understanding that she didn't

want to talk about last night in front of Léelk'w. "Good. Well, I'd better start my day."

He lingered, as if he wanted to say something more, but then looked over his shoulder at Léelk'w and walked into his room.

Evelyn made sure that he'd closed his door before she turned back to Léelk'w. "You chased him off."

Léelk'w snorted. "He doesn't like me much, but he's a good doctor."

"Why do you give him a hard time, then?"

"I give *all* doctors a hard time." Léelk'w fixed her with a serious gaze, but there was a twinkle in her eyes. "I gave your father a hard time at first."

"I see." Evelyn ignored that, trying not to think of her father, and picked up Jennifer's chart just as Jennifer and Joe Jr. came into the clinic.

"Dr. Saunders! No laboring women today?" Jennifer teased good-naturedly.

Evelyn smiled. "Not today. I'm all yours."

"Léelk'w, I wasn't expecting to see you here," Jennifer said in surprise.

"I am here, and you will give Dr. Saunders permission to speak with me, yes?"

"Of course," Jennifer said, and then turned to

Evelyn. "It's okay if Léelk'w knows about my file."

"Okay, but I'll only discuss your file with her in front of you. I'm bound by rules of doctor-patient confidentiality."

Jennifer winked and Evelyn saw Joe Jr. was trying not to laugh.

"Okay, let's get you to the exam room. I want to take another look at your baby and see how he or she is growing."

"Sounds good!" Jennifer said excitedly as she got up and walked toward Evelyn.

They knew where they were going, and Janet was waiting for them in the exam room that held the ultrasound.

As Léelk'w passed Evelyn she squeezed her shoulder.

Evelyn took a deep breath.

You can do this. This is no different from any other patient with intrauterine growth restriction. This isn't your family.

Not anymore.

Only it was. This was her cousin's wife.

This was technically her family, but solely by genetics.

Evelyn had been on her own too long.

She didn't have family. She just had herself.

And that was all she deserved.

Derek had wanted to get to work early so as to avoid Evelyn, but then he'd run smack-dab into her. He felt like a fool, thinking that perhaps he'd led her on and now she'd be clingy, but of course she wasn't. She was trying to avoid him just as much as he'd been trying to avoid her.

Even though he should be relieved he was quite upset by that, because he wanted her. He didn't want Evelyn to have to avoid him or vice versa.

He wanted more and that thought scared him.

What is wrong with you? Isn't that what you wanted?

Except maybe it wasn't.

When they'd collided this morning he'd been glad to see her, his body instantly reacting to her.

When he was younger and had felt that way he would usually sleep with the woman to work her out of his system. Then he'd met Vivian and those roguish ways of his youth had disappeared. Vivian had been the only one for him.

Yeah, and she's dead. She's been gone for five years.

Derek groaned and scrubbed a hand over his

face. He'd sworn when Vivian had died and torn open his heart that he would never allow himself ever to think of another woman that way again. Yet here he was, doing just the opposite. What was wrong with him?

Well, whatever was going on with him he had to get control of it.

There was a knock at his office door.

"Come," he said, regaining his composure.

Evelyn opened the door. That glorious dark auburn hair that was just as soft as he'd imagined it to be was tied back.

Seriously, dude. Get a grip.

"Do you have a moment?" she asked.

"Yeah, sure."

She slipped inside and shut the door, crossing her arms and frowning as she stood there. "It's Jennifer Yazzie."

Derek's heart sank. "She has intrauterine growth restriction, doesn't she?"

Evelyn closed her head and nodded.

"Damn," he cursed. "What's your course of action?"

"Monitor weekly. I explained kick counts and put her on bed-rest. So far the baby looks to be doing well, but it is small for gestational age. I don't think it would survive the stress of a vaginal delivery, so at thirty-five weeks I want to get to her Sitka and do a C-section. In the Sitka hospital they have a great NICU and that's the baby's best chance. Did she ever have rubella as a child?"

"Jennifer? No, she didn't have rubella. She was vaccinated."

"And all the tox screens come back clean?"

Derek frowned. "She's a good kid...er...woman. She doesn't smoke or drink or anything like that—as we discussed before."

"I know, but I'm trying to rule out reasons for intrauterine growth restriction. I think there might be something chromosomal going on, and it could be the baby."

"You want to do an amniocentesis, don't you?"

Evelyn nodded. "I want to test the baby's lung maturity and whether the baby will require blood transfusions. Also, Jennifer is RH negative. I would like to administer Rhogam as she lost her first pregnancy at twenty weeks."

"Right, I do remember that."

Evelyn nodded. "So there are a lot of factors that put her in the high-risk category. Not to mention the intrauterine growth restriction."

"Has she given permission for you to do an amniocentesis."

"She has, but you don't have the right gauge needle in stock. Nor do you have Rhogam. Sitka can't take her—their genetic department is overloaded and they don't currently have any Rhogam. But Juneau does, so I want to go to Juneau and get what I need, then fly the sample to Sitka, where they'll test it. I'm hoping you'll let me off for a day or so to get to Juneau and back. Joe Jr. has a car I can borrow."

Derek couldn't believe he was about to offer, but he didn't want Evelyn driving to Juneau and getting lost. And he had an "in" at the Juneau hospital. He could get everything she needed—including a place to do the procedure.

"I'll take you to Juneau. I'm going there on Saturday."

"You don't have to do that. I can arrange my own transportation. I don't want you to go out of your way."

"I'm not going out of my way. I was going there anyways. Tell Joe Jr. to get Jennifer to Juneau by Sunday and I can get you access to a safe site to do the procedure. Sunday is an off day, and you'll have access to the lab."

"You can get access to the Juneau hospital?"

"Yeah, an old schoolfriend of mine is Chief of Surgery at Juneau General. I can make a call."

"What about Mo?" Evelyn asked.

"She's the reason I'm going to Juneau. My late wife's parents are there and they take Mo every other month for a couple of days. So, do you want to go? Shall I make a call to the chief?"

Evelyn grinned from ear to ear. "I'll call Jennifer and Joe right now."

Derek nodded. "Okay. Tell them to be there Sunday evening and we'll get the amnio done. Then she can rest in the hospital for a couple of days while the results come. I know she won't want to stay there if you've made arrangements in Sitka. It's hard for her family to get there."

"Well, if it's a danger to the baby the Juneau obstetrician can handle it."

Derek cocked an eyebrow. "You mean Dr. Pearson? *He's* the head of obstetrics."

Evelyn frowned. "Well, I guess I will have to go back to deliver the baby, then, if she's told to stay put. I hope Dr. Pearson is around Sunday. I would like to speak to him. Thanks, Derek."

Evelyn left the room and he shook his head, chuckling to himself as he thought about the fire and brimstone that Evelyn was going rain down on Dr. Pearson's head if she ever got hold of him.

Another reason why he liked her so much. She didn't seem to back down or shy away from uncomfortable situations, and she was willing to go above and beyond the call of duty to help her patients. *His* patients.

If she had been any other obstetrician he knew that she would have just packed the patient off to Juneau or Sitka and had the obstetrical team there deal with it. But not Evelyn. She was so involved in taking care of her patients.

She would be the perfect physician for this town.

Come on—a surgeon of her caliber, specializing in maternal fetal medicine, is not going to stay in some rinky-dink town.

Janet opened the door. She looked panicked.

"Janet, what's wrong?"

"It's Mr. Schilling. He was out on his fishing trawler and there's been an accident. The trawler is about five minutes out and they're going to bring him here to get him stabilized before even attempting to fly him to Sitka."

Derek leapt up and grabbed his jacket. "What happened?"

"I don't know. They didn't say."

"I'm headed there, Janet. Tell Dispatch at the docks that I'm coming."

"I restocked the blood supply while I was in Sitka. Don't forget that," Janet said as she left the room.

Derek went into the supply room and began to grab things he might possibly need for a trauma. Including a cooler with the blood.

He couldn't think about Evelyn right now, or the fact that she'd be gone by the end of three months. One of his patients needed him.

And that was why he stayed.

It was what kept him going.

CHAPTER EIGHT

IT WAS EARLY Saturday morning, and even though Mo was extremely excited to be spending a couple of nights with her grandma and grandpa it was still too early in the morning for her. She was not an early riser, and for that Derek was extremely grateful.

It had made all those feedings in the middle of the night that much easier on him because she'd let him sleep in. Not that he'd got much sleep in the days after Vivian had died. He had just existed, because he'd had to for Mo, but sleep had been elusive and he'd only slept when his body had collapsed.

Still, Mo would fall asleep again today, which meant the three-hour trip to the ferry terminal would be so much easier. Right now she was chattering happily about Evie coming with them to Juneau.

"Will she come back with us when we come home, Daddy?"

"Of course. I'm her ride."

"Good. I like her. Do *you* like her?"

The question caught him off guard. "Yes, she's nice."

"Yes. She's super-nice."

"Mo, you barely know her—why do you like her so much?" he asked, curious.

"She's the same as me," Mo said.

"How so?"

"I don't know. She's just like me."

And that was the last thing Mo said before she fell asleep in her booster seat.

Derek was surprised at how easily Mo had taken to Evelyn. Mo was usually shy with strangers, but not Evelyn. It would hurt her when Evelyn left. He had to make sure Mo understood that Evelyn wasn't here to stay.

Evelyn was waiting in front of the clinic with a small bag for the overnight stay and a tray with two coffees from Sally and a small box.

Derek parked the car but left it running as he got out and took her bag from her, putting it in the trunk next to his and Mo's luggage.

Evelyn slipped into the front seat and Derek closed the trunk, returning to the driver's seat.

"She's asleep," Evelyn whispered, peering into the back seat.

"Yeah, she's not a morning person."

Evelyn set the coffee into the cup-holders, but held onto the box. "I bought her some chocolate chip cookies."

"Well, it's a long trip. They'll keep. Chocolate in the morning? Would you enjoy a three-hour car ride listening to an endless stream of shrieking?"

She laughed quietly. "Yeah, well, Sally said they were her favorite."

"Thanks—and for the coffee. It's appreciated, but unnecessary."

He pulled out onto the main road and headed out of town to the dense forest road that wound its way through the island and headed for the ferry terminal in Hoonah. From there it would be another three hours or so until the ferry docked in Jordan Springs and then it was a short drive to Juneau.

"So who is going to watch the practice for the couple days we're gone?"

"There's a young resident who flies in from Sitka when I need to make a Juneau run. I scheduled this trip long before you showed up. He arrived the same night as I set Mr. Schilling's leg. Dr. Vance has family here."

Evelyn winced. "I heard about Mr. Schilling's accident, but Janet didn't tell me everything and we've been so busy at the clinic since."

"Well, he got a hook in his hand, and just as he was about to get it out a wave struck the side of his trawler. A boom wasn't fastened properly and it came down on his leg. He's lucky it wasn't crushed. But it was a pretty simple break and I stitched up the hand."

"For a fish hook?"

Derek chuckled. "It's not some angler's fish hook you can buy at the store and use at the old fishing hole, Evelyn. It was a large commercial fish hook."

Evelyn winced again. "Okay. Got it. I don't need to hear anymore."

Derek chuckled. "That makes you queasy?"

"Yeah, your description of it *does* make me queasy. This is why I didn't pursue trauma surgery. It's not my forte. I can lend a hand in a trauma situation, but fish hooks…no, thanks."

He grinned and then shook his head. "It's a way of life up here."

"I know. My dad was the doctor here and… I remember some interesting accidents."

"Like what?"

Evelyn shook her head. "I'm really not going to talk about them."

"Come on," he teased.

She shuddered. "Fish hooks were some, I guess. But the most interesting one was a bear mauling."

"I've had one of those."

"Oh. Was it a tourist?"

"Yes," he said in surprise. "How did you know?"

"They get in too close to the wildlife. I remember Dad talking about it. It used to frustrate him, because once a bear loses its fear of a human it ends up getting destroyed. It was a pet peeve of his."

"I get that."

They didn't say anything else, but he knew that Evelyn understood the way of life up here. It was nice that she *got* it. That he didn't have to explain things to her. She just *knew* and he could talk to her openly about life up close to the sixtieth parallel. Which was so different from anywhere else—except further north, perhaps.

I wish she'd stay.

And that thought caught him off guard.

"Anyways, Mr. Schilling will make a full recovery. He's at home for the rest of the season and Dr. Vance will check in on him while we're gone," Derek said, changing the subject.

"Your replacement?"

Derek nodded. "I was hoping he'd take a permanent position in Wolf's Harbor, but I don't think he will. He has a girlfriend in Sitka. I just need a couple of regular doctors to help with my bid to get funding for a hospital in Wolf's Harbor."

"If you had a hospital I wouldn't have to go to Juneau to run this test, or send Jennifer so far away from Wolf's Harbor to have her baby."

"Exactly. Wolf's Harbor is right in the middle of the Inside Passage and we serve a lot of fishermen and loggers. I've been trying since I lost my first patient over a preventable injury when I first came here."

"What happened?" Evelyn asked.

"Cut his femoral artery in a logging accident. If I could've gotten him into surgery we might have saved him. But I can't get surgeons or nurses to stay in Wolf's Harbor."

Evelyn didn't respond to that, but he saw the

bloom of color in her cheeks as she went back to looking out the window.

Great. This is going to be a fun three hours. What else can we talk about to make it completely awkward for her?

"Ever been to Juneau before?" he asked, trying to steer the conversation to something more chatty.

"No. I've never been to Juneau…well, other than to the airport when I was sent to live with my grandmother in Boston. I went to Sitka and then flew to Juneau and then to Boston, which was a long flight."

"You don't like flying?" he asked.

"No."

The silence fell between them again. He felt awkward, nervous around her.

Then Derek chuckled. "I'm sorry."

"For what?"

"I can't seem to start a conversation without it getting awkward."

Evelyn grinned. "I know. Let's stick to talking about Juneau, because I've been to Hoonah, and my dad would take me sometimes to watch the cruise ships come up the Inside Passage or we'd watch for whales, but I've never taken the ferry to Juneau."

"Never?"

"Never. Dad would take the ferry to Juneau if he needed to go to the hospital, but I would always remain behind with Léelk'w."

"Léelk'w means grandmother?" he asked.

"It's what I called her. Or what she told me to call her. Do you know much Tlingit?"

"No. I don't know much. I've had people try to teach me, but no."

"You've been in Wolf's Harbor for—what?—fifteen years?—and you don't know much Tlingit?"

"Well, I haven't had much time to learn it, and languages are not my forte, much to my mother's chagrin."

"Your mother wanted you to speak a lot of languages?"

"She is Haitian and my dad was Ukrainian, but I couldn't pick up any of the languages my parents spoke—not Haitian Creole, not French, and certainly not Ukrainian or Russian. My Spanish grades in school were miserable too."

Evelyn chuckled. "Well, Léelk'w would speak

to me when I was younger in Tlingit. Dad didn't know much. He did know Russian, though."

"Do *you* know Russian?"

"No," she said. "Just English, Tlingit, French and Spanish."

Derek snorted. "Show off."

Evelyn laughed, her eyes twinkling. He liked it when she smiled at him. It made him feel good. It made him feel at ease and relaxed. It made him feel alive again.

"You have a pretty smile, you know."

She smirked. "So do you. Although I was kind of used to your scowling."

Derek chuckled. "Thanks."

"So, tell me more about Juneau and this ferry ride. I mean, it's a three-hour ferry ride, yes?"

"Yep, but the views are incredible, and the ferry has a cafeteria on board, a movie lounge and a lot of comfortable seating."

"Wow! I'm impressed."

"What did you think it was going to be like?"

"I thought it would be like a barge."

"Nah, we do things right here in Alaska—come on—it's a three-and-half-hour voyage."

"It's very good of your friend to offer us space to do this test. Really it should've been done ages ago. I really hope I *do* have a run-in with this Dr. Pearson."

Derek cocked an eyebrow. "What're you going to do to him?"

"What do you mean?" she asked, confused.

"You sound like some kind of cowboy character, out for revenge. Are you going to deck him or something?" he teased.

"Tempting, but, no. I am going to question his medical integrity."

"That's the same as shouting *Draw!* in the Old West."

Evelyn snorted. "Well, whatever, but he messed up when it came to two patients. Christina and Jennifer. At least Christina survived—as did her baby."

"And Jennifer's will survive. You're here."

Evelyn gave him hope. Something he hadn't felt in so long. And he wanted to pull her into his arms and tell her how alive she made him feel, but he couldn't.

And he didn't want to think about the next doctor coming in. One who wouldn't measure up to Evelyn, because none before had been like her.

Evelyn's expression softened. "Yes."

"Look, he didn't care. He was forced to go on that rotation, like most are. He didn't take it seriously. No one ever does. They just see a small town on a remote side of an island far from civilization."

"I know, but I still want to give him a piece of my mind."

"Okay, but don't step on any toes," Derek warned.

He didn't want to jeopardize the rotation of professionals to Wolf's Harbor, but honestly, if it came right down to it, he was going to back Evelyn every step of the way when it came to dealing with Dr. Pearson.

The rest of their trip to Hoonah passed peacefully. Mo slept the entire time until they got into the line-up of vehicles waiting for passage. That was when she woke up, and was more than happy to have the cookie that Evelyn offered her.

It wasn't a long wait before Derek drove his car into the vehicle hold of the ferry. Evelyn grabbed her bag out of the trunk, Derek grabbed what he needed for Mo and they headed to the upper decks.

Once they were in the solarium Mo ran straight

for the lounge chairs that were closest to the prow of the ferry and overlooked the open water of the Inside Passage and the mountains that seemed completely to surround them.

"Wow," Evelyn whispered. "I forgot."

"What?" Derek asked, taking off his jacket and setting it down on one of the chairs.

"What it looked like." There was a sparkle in her eyes as she drank it all in. "I really forgot what it looked like. I think I'm going to head out on deck."

Derek nodded and watched her go. Mo wanted to stay in the comfy chairs, where she could stand and look out the window as she didn't like the wind blowing in her face. So he stayed with Mo and watched Evelyn through the window. He couldn't help but watch her as she leaned over the rail, the wind coming off the water tangling her hair around her face.

She was wiping tears away.

His heart melted for her and he was terrified by how much she moved him. How she was making him feel again.

Something he hadn't ever thought would ever happen again.

Something he didn't want to happen again.

* * *

Evelyn had to regain her composure.

She'd forgotten about this place.

She'd forgotten about the times her father had taken her to Hoonah and how she would stare for hours at the mountains and the water. She'd forgotten what it looked like. The picture in her mind hadn't done justice to what she was actually looking at.

She closed her eyes and drank in the salty smell of the water, the mist that clung in the air on this gray morning.

"Look, see that over there?" her father said, pointing as they stood on the pier.

"What, Daddy?" She glanced over, but could only see water.

"Watch for it."

A jet of water spouted from the surface and she saw a smooth, effortless black back just peek out of the water.

"Oh! What is that?"

"An orca pod. See—there are several of them. They travel together. They're a family."

Evelyn smiled and squeezed his hand. "Mommy loved orcas."

Her dad nodded solemnly. "She did. She loved them so much."

"I love them too. I will love them forever, and when I see them I'll think of Mommy."

Her dad hugged her tight and kissed the top of her head.

"Yes. Do that. That is what she would want you to do. She dreamed of her spirit roaming free over these waters with them."

The horn from the ferry startled her. She quickly wiped away her tears and looked back.

Mo was in the window, waving at her and Derek was gazing at her, a strange look on his face. Their gaze locked for a brief moment and then he looked away.

Evelyn took a deep breath and headed back into the solarium as the ferry began to pull away from the docks, leaving Hoonah behind, headed to Juneau on the far side of the passage.

"Hey, Evie!" Mo shrieked, bouncing up and down in her seat.

Evelyn resisted the urge to hug her. She didn't want to overstep her boundaries with Derek. She knew he was protective of his daughter, and rightly so.

"Hi! Did you have a good sleep?"

"Yep!" Mo said, and then went back to her book, sitting with her legs crossed in the air as she read her alphabet story book.

Evelyn couldn't help but chuckle.

"You okay?" Derek asked.

"Fine. I just needed some fresh air, but it's kind of drizzly out there so I came back in. The water is a bit choppy today."

"Hopefully the sun will come out. After I get Mo settled with her grandparents we can take a trip up the gondola to the summit of Mount Roberts."

"A gondola ride?"

"Sure. You said you've never been to Juneau, and we have some time to kill before we meet with the chief for dinner and discuss our plan of attack at the hospital tomorrow."

"It's nice you want to entertain me, but I don't want to take you away from your family."

"You're not. You're doing me a favor. My in-laws are nice people, and great grandparents to Mo, but they were never fans of me."

Evelyn was intrigued. "Why is that?"

"I took their daughter away," he muttered under his breath. "Although truthfully she was already gone. She came to Wolf's Harbor. I didn't meet her in Juneau and whisk her away. She was trying to escape them. Vivian was a bit of a free spirit."

There was a pained sense of longing in his voice and Evelyn was envious, because she'd never felt that way about anyone ever—because she'd never let herself.

"Well, then, yes—I wouldn't mind a gondola ride to the summit of Mount Roberts. I think that might be fun. I've never been up a mountain."

He smirked. "You're born and raised in Alaska and you've never been up a mountain. Pathetic."

"Ha-ha."

"Don't fight," Mo chirped from behind her book.

They both laughed at that.

"Who's hungry?" Evelyn asked.

"Me!" Evie shouted, putting her book in her knapsack.

"Let's get some lunch. We can come back after and see if we can see some whales in the water."

Mo grinned and took Derek's hand. "Sounds good!"

Evelyn picked up her bag and they made their way to the cafeteria. Derek and Mo were walking ahead and her heart skipped a beat, aching with a sense of longing to belong. To have family.

were very strict with Vivian. At least they're a bit more relaxed with Mo, and Mo loves them both to death."

Evelyn smiled as she gazed at Mo. Her curly light brown hair fanned her round cheeks, and her lips were parted as she breathed in her sleep.

"She's a great kid."

Derek beamed proudly. "Thanks. I'm going to miss her while she's gone."

"She goes every other month?"

"In the summer. In the winter it's harder, and my in-laws usually go down south for the winter. I don't know how many more years they're going to be able to do this, or even if they'll stay in Alaska, so I want Mo to have as much time with them as possible. It's a connection to her mother."

Evelyn nodded sadly. "That's important. I had Léelk'w to remind me of *my* mother. I didn't even know about my father's mother until he passed and she gained custody of me."

"And she didn't let you keep in contact with your family up here?"

Evelyn sighed. "No, apparently not, according to Uncle Yazzie. And Grandma told me that they didn't want anything to do with me."

What she didn't say was that she'd thought they didn't want her because of her father's death. She'd taken away Wolf's Harbor's only doctor. Everyone had loved her dad. Now she wasn't sure that it was true. Still, it was hard to forgive herself...which was why she was here in Wolf's Harbor. To seek forgiveness.

The child in her had believed that they hadn't written. The adult knew they had. Her grandmother's hardened heart toward anything connected with her father's death meant she'd probably hidden the letters from her. Her grandmother had been so determined not to be reminded of her son in any way, Evelyn was surprised she'd tolerated *her* presence.

Derek started the engine and slowly drove out of the ferry. "She actually told you that?"

"Well, she put it politely. I wrote letters to Léelk'w and I guess they were never sent—and of course I never received any letters. It hurt then, but now I understand. There were legal battles fought and lost. And after a time I forgot it all. Forgot about Wolf's Harbor *and* them."

Did you?

She wasn't sure that she had.

"You didn't forget. You just buried it deep down. I get that."

They shared a look, but then Evelyn broke the gaze to look out the window as they drove down the gangway and onto land. Once they were out of the ferry terminal they turned onto the Glacier Highway and headed toward Juneau.

Mo was snoring gently in the back.

"You know, Léelk'w told me I had built up walls," Evelyn remarked.

"I think we all have our own set of walls," Derek said offhandedly.

"You have walls?"

He gave her a look and she laughed at the absurdity of the comment. Of *course* Derek had walls. She could see them as she peered over from behind her own walls. Walls were for protection. They guarded the heart.

"I have Mo to protect, and my practice. It makes it easier to deal with the stress of it all."

"Yeah." Walls were good for that too.

"So why do you think your grandmother wanted to cut you off from Wolf's Harbor?" he asked absently.

"My grandmother hated Alaska. Hated that it took her son away, wrecked all her plans for him.

The life she wanted for him. She was grieving, I suppose, in the only way she knew how. Talking about Alaska or Dad was frowned on. She only talked about my father when she expressed her disappointment in his life choices."

"Not fair to you."

Evelyn shrugged. "I know, but I get it. I get her grief."

"Grieving I get," Derek said. "Still, it must've been hard for you, not being able to talk about your family. Do you know much about your mother's family?"

"I don't remember much. Except one thing." She chuckled.

"Oh?" he asked, intrigued.

"There's a lot of Russian on my mother's side, on top of the Tlingit. My maternal grandmother had a torrid love affair with a Russian fisherman. My mother is my uncle Yazzie's half sister. So I have no idea about my maternal grandfather. Or at least my biological one."

"Hey, close to the Ukraine," he teased, and she laughed. "Torrid, eh?"

"Yeah, though I don't like to think about Léelk'w having any kind of torrid *anything*."

Derek laughed. "Yeah, I can't picture Katlian

as a young woman, but it doesn't surprise me one bit that her and her sister were a bit of a... Well, they had fun."

Evelyn laughed. "I'm glad you're letting Mo still have a connection to her mother, and I hope for Mo's sake it continues for a while longer."

She knew all too well the pain of losing your connection with everything you knew. Your heritage, everyone you loved. It was horrible, and no one should ever have to go through the pain of losing a piece of their soul.

"Me too," Derek admitted.

It didn't take them long to reach Derek's in-laws. Evelyn stayed in the car and Derek made a couple of trips to bring in the luggage that Mo needed for her couple of nights with her grandparents.

Mo gave Evelyn a hug before she left, and Evelyn cherished those small arms wrapped around her neck in a hug that had completely caught her off guard but was appreciated all the same.

Once Mo was settled, Derek returned to the car. "You ready for a trip to the summit?"

"I suppose..."

"Come on! Your *léelk'w* has an adventurous spirit. You need to have one too."

"I do have an adventurous spirit."

"Then there's no problem," Derek teased.

It wasn't a long drive to the center of Juneau's cruise ship dock. There were a couple of large ships in the harbor, but Derek parked and was able to get tickets for the next trip up in the Goldbelt Mount Roberts Tramway.

They crammed onto the tram with all the other people on their trip. It was a bit of crush, and most of the people were tourists from the cruise ships. Evelyn found herself crammed in a corner, with Derek pressed against her.

Evelyn craned her neck and saw the cables disappear almost vertically up the side of the mountain into the mist.

"Oh, my God," she whispered. "We're going up *that*?"

Derek looked. "Yep. It's eighteen hundred feet up and it's one of the most vertical tramways in the world."

She closed her eyes. "Remind me to murder you if we survive this."

"You can hold on to me—or to the hand-holds."

Evelyn went to reach for one, but an older man in front of her grabbed it, not noticing her. Derek reached down and wrapped a strong arm around her, pulling her close as he held onto a hand-hold himself. His arm around her gave her a sense of security she hadn't felt in so long.

It was nice.

The door shut and the tram began to move out of the station and up through the mist and the rainforest that blanketed the lower elevation around the mountain, on their way to the subalpine eco system at the summit.

Evelyn opened her eyes and braved the view as Juneau disappeared below them and they rose above the mist that was clinging above the city. The sun came out, burning away the drizzle, and she couldn't help but stare at the beauty in wonder.

Derek chuckled. "See—it's worth it."

"If we survive to the upper station," she teased.

"Well, since we're almost there I think that's a safe bet."

Evelyn peered over to the front of the tram to see the upper tram station waiting for them. Once the tram was safely docked the doors opened. Derek and Evelyn lingered to let the other people get off first, so they weren't caught up in the mad crush of tourists.

"Want to go for a quick hike? John said he'd

meet us at the Langstrom Grill at seven o'clock. We can head up to the alpine meadow and then take the tram back down."

"Sounds good. Lead the way. I don't think I have my footing yet."

"What?" Derek asked playfully. "Come on, you, goose. This is solid ground."

"It's a *cliff*. This station is hovering over a cliff."

Derek rolled his eyes and then stomped his foot. "See—it's solid… *Whoa!* Whoa! Oh, my God, I'm going to fall off the edge of this cliff."

Evelyn punched his arm. "Ha-ha. Funny."

Derek was shaking his head and still laughing as they left the tram and headed for a path that wound its way through two-hundred-foot-tall trees up to the alpine meadow. There were a lot of tourists going there and back, but Evelyn didn't find them as overwhelming as when they were riding the tram.

In fact as they picked their way through the zigzag path away from the upper station she found it quite relaxing, though it was a bit cooler up on the summit than it was down in the city.

They stopped halfway and sat down on a bench. Through the trees she could see Juneau below them. All the brightly colored homes, and the

cruise ships that seemed like toys in the Gastineau Channel.

She sighed. "This is great."

"Got your footing back?" he teased again.

She elbowed him. "Yes. Thanks for bringing
me up here."

"No problem. I haven't been up here in a long
time. Usually I come by myself, because I have
time to kill after dropping Mo off, waiting to
catch the ferry back to Wolf's Harbor the next
day. Sometimes I take a couple days off to myself and spend it in Juneau before I go back. A
little mini-vacation."

"Your family is still in Chicago?"

"My mom is. My dad passed away two years
ago."

"I'm surprised you didn't move back to Chicago."

Derek shrugged. "Well, I love it here, and Mo
needs her grandparents."

"What about her grandma in Chicago?"

She didn't want Mo not to have contact with
her loved ones—especially the ones who wanted
her and made an effort to stay in her life.

"My mom is coming up next month to spend
several months with me, and I have siblings in

Chicago and they have kids. Mo is getting old enough that if I can get another general practitioner up here we can go back home for Christmas or something. Mom would like that."

"I hope you find someone. I wish I could help."

Derek nodded solemnly. "Yeah, I know. But you don't know where you'll end up."

"I have offers in Seattle and at the Mayo. Even in Boston. All good offers."

"So why haven't you taken one of them?" he asked.

"I'm helping out a friend."

Those gray-green eyes narrowed in disbelief. "I think it's more than that."

"Pardon?" she asked, annoyed.

"I'm sorry. I didn't mean to upset you. I didn't think it was a touchy subject."

She didn't respond to that. She didn't tell him that it was indeed a touchy subject and she didn't feel like discussing it right now.

"It's not. I'm helping out a friend. If I wasn't, I would've left the moment she said Wolf's Harbor."

"Um…didn't you find out after the fact? Like after she left?"

"Details, details." Evelyn smiled. "Come on.

Show me this alpine meadow before we have to catch our tram back down to meet with this John."

She didn't want to talk anymore. She didn't want to talk about why she was there, seeking acceptance of the never-ending guilt over her father's death. It wasn't his business. He was just her colleague. Nothing more.

She had to remember that and protect herself. Even if she wanted more.

Derek had a shower and changed his clothes into business casual for their meeting with John. When he'd called John his friend had been wary at first, thinking that Derek was going to bombard him with questions and talk about a hospital for Wolf's Harbor, but once Derek had name-dropped Dr. Evelyn Saunders, John had taken notice. He'd heard of her.

"Derek, how the heck did you land Dr. Evelyn Saunders in Wolf's Harbor?"

"She's covering for a friend."

"She's a hot commodity. What I wouldn't give to bring her on board at Juneau General, but the board wouldn't pay enough to keep her happy here."

"Well, she needs to run some tests on a patient..."

"She can use our facilities. Of course. When is she planning on coming to Juneau?"

"I'm bringing her Saturday."

"Great. We'll have dinner Saturday night at Langstrom's."

Derek had the distinct feeling that he was going to be a third wheel in this situation, but he was okay with that. This was about helping Jennifer and Joe's baby.

He waited in the lounge for Evelyn and glanced at his watch.

The elevator dinged and she walked off.

Derek had to take a step back.

He hadn't seen her dressed up before. Her dark auburn hair was swept up off her neck and a tight black shift dress clung to her curves. High heels accented her legs and her rear, and he couldn't help but tilt his head just so in order to check her out.

And although he was glad he had, as his temperature rose, suddenly he didn't feel like having dinner with a colleague. He wanted to keep her all to himself.

Hey! Get a hold of yourself.

"You look handsome," Evelyn said.

She seemed nervous too. She was wringing her hands and fidgeting.

Good.

He was glad he wasn't the only one, and it gave him a thrill to think that maybe he was affecting her just as much as she was affecting him.

At least he hoped it was that.

"I've never seen you in a suit and dress shirt. Usually you're lumbering around in a flannel shirt."

"I can say the same about you. Jeans, cotton shirts and flats. And my shirts are woolen plaid. It deals with the moisture and the rain better than flannel."

"Are you really starting a conversation about flannel right now?" she asked teasingly.

"I do believe that I am."

Evelyn laughed. "Well, this must be important. I take it Langstrom's is the nicest place in Juneau?"

"Something like that." Derek proffered his arm. "It's not far from the hotel—just down the street. We can walk."

Derek led her outside. Even though it was seven at night, the summer's midnight sun was out—

which was too bad, because the twinkling lights down by the water were a sight to see. But it was nice to see the mountains and the water in the Gastineau Channel, which was like a mirror reflecting the mountains. At least it was early in the summer still. They wouldn't have sun till midnight quite yet.

A horn sounded from one of the cruise ships, and music was blasting from another onboard party, but it didn't ruin the beauty of the evening.

Summer in Alaska was his favorite time of year. Though there were times when he missed those endless summers in Chicago. He missed the heat, the beach, and the complete freedom he'd felt back then, when his heart had been open wide and not closed. Not so full of responsibility.

Still, he loved Mo with all his heart, and Alaska and his patients, but it would be nice not to carry the burden of all the things he was—to let loose and be who he used to be.

Derek held open the door and Evelyn stepped inside.

Langstrom's was dark. It had plush leather booths, and wide windows that overlooked the yacht club and the water. The walls were painted burgundy and the exposed beams only added to the ambiance.

He'd always liked this place. But if it had just been him coming to meet John for dinner he seriously doubted that they would've been dining here. They would've probably met at the hotel bar.

John was pulling out the big guns, and since dinner was on him and the hospital board, Derek wasn't going to object.

The maître d' led them toward a private booth tucked in the corner, and as they wound their way through happy diners Derek's heart sank as he saw that Dr. Mark Pearson was at the table.

Oh. No.

At first all he felt was a sense of dread at the thought of Evelyn and Mark meeting, but then he thought that this might be an interesting dinner indeed, and relished the idea of Evelyn putting Mark in his place.

John stood up and seemed practically giddy. Mark, the creep, was eyeing Evelyn as if she was the main course, and Derek instinctively put his hand in the small of her back, which made Evelyn take a tiny intake of breath.

And that little sound coming from her responding to his touch made his blood heat.

"Derek—so glad that you and Dr. Saunders could make it."

"I'm happy you're accommodating us, John." Derek shook John's hand and then turned to Evelyn. "Evelyn, this is Dr. John Collins, Chief of Surgery at Juneau General."

"A pleasure," Evelyn said, gripping his hand and shaking it firmly.

"The pleasure is all mine, Dr. Saunders," John gushed.

"Please call me, Evelyn."

John grinned again and turned to Mark. "Derek, I know you're familiar with Mark— Evelyn, this is Dr. Mark Pearson, Head of Obstetrics at Juneau General."

The warm, friendly smile instantly disappeared from Evelyn's face as Mark, totally unaware, took her hand.

"A pleasure, Dr. Saunders. I've been reading your work for years."

Evelyn kept the cool, fake smile on her face. "Have you really? Could've fooled me."

Derek coughed, clearing his throat and trying not to laugh as Mark looked thoroughly confused and John seemed completely oblivious to the burn directed at his head of obstetrics.

"Let's take a seat, shall we?" Derek suggested, and slid into the booth next to Mark rather than letting Evelyn sit there, which he knew Pearson was not impressed about.

"We're absolutely thrilled, Evelyn, that you're going to be using our facilities on Sunday. Everything is at your disposal."

"Thank you, John. I really shouldn't have to be doing this testing so late in the patient's pregnancy, but the last doctor who was in charge of this case was lacking."

Mark's eyes narrowed and Derek stifled another laugh.

"Well, it is hard in these smaller communities to get proper assistance when needed," said John.

Now it was Derek's turn to grind his teeth as John gave him this jab.

"Oh, Dr. Taylor has been wonderful. I honestly don't know how he manages to run things so smoothly and skillfully on his own. The town needs a hospital and more staff for sure," Evelyn said. "No, the fault of this patient falling through the cracks lies solely with the rotating OB/GYNs."

"How did you come to *that* conclusion, Dr. Saunders?" Mark asked tersely.

"I came to that conclusion because I have a patient who is documented as having intrauterine growth restriction, and yet she was never informed of that suspicion and an amniocentesis wasn't performed at twenty weeks. She's now at thirty-two weeks."

John frowned and Mark gritted his teeth.

"Perhaps an amnio would've put the patient in danger—and perhaps that patient didn't follow doctor's orders and get herself to Sitka or Juneau to have it taken care of with proper genetic counsellors?"

Evelyn smiled and picked up her menu. "Perhaps. But something should've been done before this."

Derek was having the best time. He loved her sense of humor and he especially loved watching Dr. Mark Pearson squirm in his seat. Evelyn was smart, she had an edge, and he was really enjoying this interchange.

"What's good here?" Evelyn asked, directing her question to John, who looked relieved to turn the conversation away from talking about Mark's error.

* * *

It took every ounce of Evelyn's strength during that long dinner not to reach across the table and throttle Dr. Mark Pearson for so many reasons, but she didn't want to embarrass Derek or John, who was a lovely man.

She was very aware that she was being wooed by this hospital, but she wasn't interested in Juneau General. Not if it meant that she had to work with Dr. Pearson. Perhaps he was a capable OB/GYN, but his mismanagement of two patients in Wolf's Harbor put a sour taste in her mouth.

The dinner was delicious, and she was glad to be treated to lobster and wine. She was even more glad that she would have the full run of all the hospital's facilities.

She'd received a text from Joe Jr. in the middle of the meal that stated he and Jennifer were in Hoonah for the night, so they wouldn't have to spend all day on the road, and Evelyn had texted back that it was a smart decision.

"Well, gentleman, it's been an absolute pleasure, but it's been a long day and I have to prepare for a very risky amniocentesis tomorrow." Evelyn stood up and the men followed suit.

"I look forward to seeing you tomorrow," John said, taking her hand.

"Thank you, John," said Derek, shaking John's hand next.

Mark just nodded, but didn't say anything as she slid out of the booth, completely satisfied that she'd put the pompous ass in his place.

Derek slid out after her and guided her through the restaurant.

They didn't say anything until they were outside, but when they were a few feet from the restaurant Evelyn started laughing uncontrollably, as did Derek. It eased the tension between them that had become almost palpable.

"Evelyn, that dinner…that was worth the drive to Juneau," Derek said through his laughing. "Mark's face, it was priceless. I love karma."

"It was good, wasn't it?" She giggled. "I didn't know he was going to be there."

"Neither did I. I swear. I was worried you were going to deck him."

"I wanted to, believe me," Evelyn muttered. "He was brought there as bait."

"Bait?"

"I'm a woman," she said astutely.

Derek grinned lazily. "I'm very well aware of *that*."

Heat bloomed in her cheeks. "I mean he's a very good-looking man and he was meant to entice me. This isn't been the first time this has happened and it probably won't be the last."

"How many times has this happened to you before?"

"Twice, really. And one time it *did* work. I was with Nathan for two years."

"You don't seem sad about it," Derek remarked.

She shrugged. "It was for the best."

"You wanted different things?"

She nodded. "I wanted a career and he wanted roots, so we ended our relationship."

"I'm sorry."

"Don't be. It's fine. I've learned not to be dazzled by the best in show at a hospital."

"I hadn't noticed that about Mark before, but I suppose he is. So, would you have been enticed if it hadn't been Dr. Pearson?"

"Nope. I'm not swayed that way. They can try, but I've learned my lesson."

"Good," he said, and slipped his arm around her. It felt natural.

It was darker out—the start of a few scant

hours of darkness. It wasn't completely summer yet. The end of June would bring about the really long days.

Evelyn stared up at the sky. Just over the harbor there was the faint ripple of the northern lights, but the dwindling dusk and city lights obscured them, stopping the truly stunning display they could've made.

"Oh," she whispered, staring up at them in awe. "I'd forgotten about them too. It's been so long."

"They're beautiful. I never tire of them," he said dreamily.

"Léelk'w told me they're the spirits of the departed dancing."

"I heard you're supposed to whistle at them to make them dance."

Evelyn frowned. "But I heard that some Inuit in Canada believe whistling at them means the spirits will come down and grab you. Don't whistle."

"Okay. I wouldn't want to be grabbed."

Evelyn chuckled. "No, neither would I."

They stood there in silence, just staring up at the green ripple of northern lights, his arm still around her.

It had felt so good when he'd placed his arm

around her, and when his hand had been in the small of her back. Maybe it was the wine talking, but if Derek had been the bait, and if she'd been a different person, then she would have jumped at the job John was so slyly offering her.

Evelyn took a step forward, and before she knew what was happening she was lost in those gray-green eyes and swept up into a kiss that was tender at first but then, as she melted into his arms, became more intense. It felt so right, so good.

What are you doing? This isn't smart.

She broke off the kiss and pushed him away. "Sorry," she said breathlessly.

Derek glanced down at her, saw her staring up at him. "What?"

Embarrassed, she looked away. "Nothing— just tired."

Chicken.

"Okay, let's get back to the hotel so you can get some rest. It'll be a busy day tomorrow."

Evelyn nodded and they walked back to the hotel. His arm was by his side, the magic of the moment broken, but it was good that it had been shattered.

Derek was off limits.

She just wished she could remember that and stop testing fate.

CHAPTER TEN

EVELYN SPENT THE day mostly by herself, getting ready for Jennifer's arrival at the hospital in the afternoon, because there were no staff in Patient Intake working on a Sunday and she had refused to let John call one in. She'd told Joe to text her when they arrived so that she could meet them in the lobby and explain everything.

She hadn't seen Derek in the morning, but she'd left him a note at the front desk to let him know that she'd taken a cab over to the hospital. That kiss was still burned onto her lips, but she was nervous about seeing him. She wasn't sure if she'd be able to control herself around him. His kiss had made her completely melt and she wanted more. So much more.

It was for the best that she ignored him and focused on work.

That was why she was here.

Dr. Pearson had made himself scarce, and she

was glad for that. The resident she'd been assigned was more than capable.

She had the NICU team on standby, and an operating room available to her should she need it, but she was hoping that she wouldn't.

Sometimes there was no reason at all for intrauterine growth restriction, and even though the baby would be born prematurely, with some health complications, there was still a very high chance that the baby would grow up to be a healthy adult.

That was if there was no chromosomal inconsistencies in this amniotic fluid draw, and Evelyn was really hoping that there wasn't.

Her phone buzzed and she saw that Joe had sent a message to say that they were in the lobby. Evelyn took one last look around the exam room where she'd be doing the work and then made her way down.

As it was Sunday the main lobby of the hospital was pretty empty because there were no scheduled procedures. It was the other side of the hospital that housed the emergency room, and that was always busy.

Jennifer was in a wheelchair, and Evelyn breathed a sigh of relief when she saw that. It meant that Jennifer was taking her advice on bed-rest.

"Joe, Jennifer, I'm so glad you made it."

Joe nodded, and Jennifer was smiling, but Evelyn could tell she was scared out of her mind.

"Thanks for doing this, Evie," Joe said.

"It's no problem. I'm just glad we're able to do it—and so quickly. I'm sorry it's so far from Wolf's Harbor, but this is for the best."

"Well, I'm ready if the baby needs to be delivered today," Jennifer said nervously.

Evelyn took her hand and felt Jennifer's fingers tremble in hers. "I do this all the time. We'll check on the baby, and if he or she is doing well we'll try to keep him or her in there as long as we can. But I do plan on delivering your baby at thirty-five weeks. That's my current choice. So week thirty-four we'll get you to Sitka, yes? You can wait it out in the hospital and then I'll come and perform a C-section."

"It *has* to be a C-section?" Jennifer asked with trepidation.

"Your baby is measuring very small, and I'm not sure it would survive the trauma of a vaginal birth. It's for the best, and I promise you it's not as bad as it seems."

Joe pushed the chair, following Evelyn through the hospital.

She could tell that Jennifer was nervous, and couldn't even begin to imagine what she was going through. Over a year ago Jennifer had lost a baby, quite far along, and now this.

Evelyn was going to do everything in her power to make sure this baby lived. As she did with all her patients.

"How long do we have to stay in Juneau?" Jennifer asked as they rode the elevator up to the obstetrical floor.

"Only a couple of days," Evelyn said. "We just want to make sure that you don't go into preterm labor. I'm sorry—this must be a hit to your business, Joe."

"Nah, Dad is covering for me."

"This is our room. Jennifer, there's a hospital gown. Change into it and I'll come back in a few minutes. This will be over before you know it, and then we'll get you into a hospital room and get you fed."

Jennifer nodded and Evelyn shut the door to give them privacy.

As she headed to the next room to get the chart

she saw Dr. Pearson headed towards her. He had a scowl on his face.

She was secretly pleased he was so put out. He was a dumb-ass and needed to be taken down a notch. She was annoyed that he was headed in her direction, though.

Great.

At least she knew how to deal with arrogant guys like him.

"Ah, Dr. Pearson. How can I help you this fine morning?" Evelyn asked sweetly, and crossed her arms to hold her ground.

"Dr. Saunders—I thought you might be a bit more gracious, given that *I* run this department. Your behavior last night—"

"Was justified," Evelyn snapped, cutting him off.

"And how do you figure *that*?" Mark growled under his breath.

"Christina. You were supposed to turn her baby the day I arrived, but you decided you wanted to head back to Juneau early. Thanks for leaving the apartment like a pigsty, by the way. I really appreciated that."

"I had more pressing matters to attend to!"

"You were supposed to wait for me and give me at least *some* information about the patients."

"Is that what you're bitter about? Because I didn't stick around and clean an apartment? You were late. I had to catch the last ferry from Hoonah."

"No, I couldn't really care less about the apartment, or the fact you're a slob. What I care about is the fact you didn't turn Christina's baby and a day later she went into labor. I had to deliver a frank breech in a clinic. Not in a hospital—in a *clinic*."

"She had time. It was her first, and the baby would've turned on its own."

"She was thirty-eight weeks. That's not a premature infant. That's almost full term."

"I couldn't have known she would go into labor early. It was her first," Mark snapped.

"That doesn't matter. It should've been done when you said you were going to do it. I delivered a frank breech and had a uterine tear. Thankfully both of them survived."

To give him credit Mark did look relieved about that fact. At least he wasn't a totally heartless jerk.

"Well, I'm glad—but the way you brought it up

last night was totally unprofessional. That's not how we handle things around here."

"Alaska is no different from any other hospital I've worked in."

Mark rolled his eyes. "Please. Alaska is not the same as the rest of the country. And Wolf's Harbor is small town—completely backward. I'm surprised you're even bothering with those people…but then again the way you and Derek were making eyes at each other last night I maybe get why you're bothering so much."

The urge to reach out and slap Dr. Pearson was strong, but she kept it in check. Still, she was worried that he'd seen something. What had Derek seen? Maybe Derek thought she was giving him a signal.

Aren't you?

Whatever it was, she knew it couldn't continue—and if other people were noticing it then Mo might notice it, and she couldn't let that happen.

"I will not humiliate you further, Dr. Pearson, but be advised that I have reported your inaction to the Alaska Health Board and the College of Physicians and Surgeons. Small town or not, the people of Wolf's Harbor matter."

Mark opened his mouth to say something further, but instead spun around on his heel and stormed off.

Evelyn took a deep breath, trying to calm her ire. Her pulse was thundering in her ears and she was still fuming.

Mark had basically written off the people of Wolf's Harbor because he felt they were backward for wanting to live a simpler life. He obviously didn't know that he was messing with a Wolf's Harbor native.

And really he didn't need to know that.

It wouldn't make any difference anyway.

She took another deep calming breath. She needed to focus. She had a job to do. A delicate procedure. And she wasn't going to let someone like that get into her head and screw it up.

Derek purposely kept away from the hospital because he didn't want to distract Evelyn.

Oh, who are you kidding? You don't want to be distracted by her.

Last night, walking her home, when they had been staring up at the northern lights all he'd wanted to do was take her in his arms and kiss her. And he'd done just that because he hadn't been able to control himself.

The scent of her hair was still burned into his brain.

The feel of her soft lips against his.

The way his blood had burned with desire for her.

How he'd wanted her even more.

And for the life of him he couldn't remember the last time he'd had so much fun. When he'd felt unburdened and free.

It was nice.

It had been a long time since he'd cut loose.

Mo's grandparents took her a lot during the summer, but he never really enjoyed himself without her. Usually, he was lonely with her gone and would work to fill the void.

He was still missing Mo, but it had been nice spending the evening with Evelyn and watching her handle the two other surgeons. It was a side of her he quite liked.

Strong-willed, stubborn and headstrong.

She had backbone and integrity.

He admired that in her.

So what was he so afraid of?

Having his heart broken again and, worse, having Mo go through the pain of losing someone she loved.

It was better to keep his distance. He must have temporarily lost his mind last night, when he'd taken her in his arms and kissed her.

He went up to the hospital to see if Evelyn wanted to have some dinner and to ask how the procedure had gone. He found her in the obstetrical patients' wing at the charge station, charting and grinding her teeth.

Derek frowned, hoping that nothing had happened to Jennifer and Joe's baby.

"Evelyn?" he said cautiously.

She glanced up and then smiled, but the smile was brief. "Oh, hey. Where have you been all day?"

"Keeping out of your hair," he said. "Is everything okay?"

"Yes, why would you…? Oh." She shook her head and *tsked* under her breath. "Just a run-in with Mark before the procedure. It set me on edge."

"How is Jennifer doing?"

"Good. She came through with flying colors. The baby's heartbeat is strong. Now I'm just waiting on the testing of the fluid. Joe and Jennifer are staying here until Wednesday, but they're in good hands if she goes into labor. We can head back to Wolf's Harbor tomorrow."

"Yeah, I got a message from Janet that there's a new pregnant patient in town and she's quite nervous."

"They always are." Evelyn chuckled. "Not that I blame them. I'd be terrified."

The words surprised him. "You don't want kids?"

"No," she said. "I like kids but…it's terrifying."

He was disappointed in her response, and then he was annoyed with himself for caring and for thinking about her constantly. What was going *on* with him?

"I came by to see if you wanted some dinner."

"I would love some," she said. "Where are you thinking?"

"The hotel restaurant? You should really get some rest before the long drive back to Wolf's Harbor. And we have to pick up Mo on our way out of town."

"Okay, let me go and make one last check on Joe and Jennifer and then I'll change out of these scrubs. It's going to take a couple of days for the labs to run the amniotic fluid. I can't sit around here waiting, though I want to. I'll be back in a few minutes."

Derek was relieved that Jennifer Yazzie had come through the procedure with flying colors, but he had never doubted that she would—not with Evelyn taking care of it.

She was such a talented surgeon.

I wish she would stay.

He cursed under his breath, angry at himself for continuing to think that way. Evelyn wasn't going to stay and he couldn't get attached even if he wanted to do just that. Surgeons like Evelyn never stayed. And how much work could Wolf's Harbor pull in for a surgeon of her caliber? Not much. They were a town of just under a thousand people. Most of that population elderly or male.

Not a huge call for OB/GYNs, even though his clinic did also serve the surrounding area. There were a lot of small villages near Wolf's Harbor.

Maybe there *would* be enough work for her. That was if he could get his small hospital off the ground.

Stop trying to find reasons for her to stay. You'll only get hurt.

"There you are. I was wondering where you'd got too."

"Just wandering. Waiting," he responded gruffly.

He *had* to get control of these thoughts.

"Are you okay?" she asked.

No.

"Yeah, fine. Let's go get something to eat."

Derek couldn't remember when he'd got so good at pretending that he was okay. It was just something he'd learned to do. Learned to cope with the fact that he'd forgotten what it was like to feel.

It was his fault that dinner was so awkward. He'd thrown those walls back up, even though he wanted to let Evelyn in. He didn't blame her when she excused herself and went to bed early. It was for the best.

The next morning was no better, but when they picked up Mo from his in-laws whatever tension there was seemed to melt away.

Or at least Evelyn acted as if there was no awkwardness between them for the benefit of Mo, which he appreciated immensely.

She was so good with Mo, and Mo just adored her. Why did this have to be so complicated?

"I can't wait to get back home," Mo chirped from the back seat.

Derek smiled as he glanced back at her in the rearview mirror, and then he looked over at Evelyn, who was smiling too, but then she frowned.

"What's going on?" she asked as they approached the ferry terminal, which seemed to have a blockade around it.

"I don't know." Derek slowed down and one of the state troopers who had clearly set up the blockade came forward when Derek stopped and rolled down his window.

"Good morning, folks. Are you headed to Hoonah?"

"Yes," Derek said. "We're on the first ferry back."

"A fog bank has rolled in from Sitka. It's pretty bad and there are no ferries operating that way at the moment."

"So what do we do?" Derek asked. "Will the ferry service resume once the fog bank clears?"

"Tomorrow. hopefully," the trooper said. "Even the planes are grounded. If you have tickets you can head to the office. They've made arrangements for accommodation for all stranded passengers."

"Thank you, Officer."

The state trooper nodded and stepped back, directing Derek where to go.

"What do we do?" Evelyn asked.

"Well, we're stuck. We'll find out what accommodation they have for us and I'll call Dr. Vance and let him know about our delay."

"Aren't we going on the boat, Daddy?" Mo asked.

"Not at the moment." Derek pulled into a parking place. "I'll go in with the tickets and find out what's going on."

Evelyn nodded. "Sure."

"I'll be back."

The line wasn't too long. The ferry terminal had everything moving swiftly and accommodation had been set up at motel further up the road that was formed of a series of small cabins. The only problem was that the three of them would have to share a cabin. There wasn't a separate cabin for Evelyn. At least the cabin had two rooms. He could stay with Mo in her room and Evelyn could have the other one. But they were stuck until the fog bank cleared, and that wasn't likely to happen until the morning.

He headed back to the car and slid in the driver side. "We have a cabin."

"A cabin?" Evelyn asked.

"That sounds like fun!" Mo said excitedly.

"Nothing to do but wait it out."

"I hope they have television," Mo said.

Evelyn shared a secret smile with him.

"Well, I was thinking we'd check into our cabin and then maybe drive up the coast to where the road ends and see if we can spot the sea lions in Point Bridget State Park."

"That sounds like fun!" Evelyn said.

Derek turned back to Mo. "Is that okay?"

"Yes!"

"Okay, sea lions it is."

It was just a short drive to the cabin motel and they checked in, dropping off their bags. There was a small café in the motel, where they grabbed a quick bite to eat and Evelyn bought some sandwiches to eat later in the park.

Driving along the coast was amazing, but they were soon headed north, toward Skagway—and there was no road to Skagway. The road ended at the beautiful, rugged Point Bridget National Park.

It had been a long time since Derek had been there, and as they all laughed and chatted on the drive up he was actually excited to go there again.

He hadn't been there since he was dating Vivian. He had always meant to bring Mo here, but had never got the chance, and then it had slipped his mind. Of course Vivian wasn't here, but he was glad he was bringing their daughter and he was glad he was sharing it with Evelyn.

When they got to the state park they took the easy three-and-a-half-kilometer trail that made its way down to the rocky shore of the Inside Passage. The mountains all around them were reflected in the crystal-clear water and it was enough to take his breath away.

Even though it was densely foggy toward Sitka, here at Point Bridget it was sunny, and as they approached the final bend down to the water they heard the barking call of the sea lions out on the large rocks, sunning themselves.

Mo squealed, but kept her distance as she picked her way across the rocky shore, with Evelyn following close behind her. They were searching for rocks—colorful rocks that had been smoothed by the tides.

Derek couldn't help but smile as he watched them.

He wanted her. He wanted Evelyn and he couldn't remember the last time he'd felt this way. It was a long time since he'd let himself feel and though he was terrified by the emotions coursing through him it was hard to ignore them. Especially now, watching her as she knelt down beside Mo, their heads together as Evelyn showed her how to skip a stone across the water.

He didn't deserve to be this happy. Only he couldn't help himself. Try as he might to stop her, Evelyn kept wiggling her way in. It was hard to push her away when she brought him to life again.

"Daddy, watch!" Mo shrieked.

Derek waved and watched as Evelyn bent over Mo and helped her skip a stone across the water. The stone bounced three times before disappearing under the water with a plop.

"Good job." Derek clapped.

"You try, Daddy," Mo said.

Derek chuckled. "Okay. I'll try."

He shook off whatever doubts were eating away at him. Right now he couldn't think about those things. Right now he was just going to enjoy this stolen moment in life, because it might be the only chance he would get before Evelyn left.

Evelyn sat down on the couch in the cabin. She felt a little sunburnt, but her shower had felt good and Derek had now retreated into the shower while Evelyn sat with Mo in the living room. Mo was in her pajamas and watching a cartoon movie. She was really quiet, and Evelyn had the feeling that Mo was exhausted.

She understood that because she was beat too. But the day had been wonderful. They'd hiked, had an impromptu picnic and watched the sea lions frolic down by the water.

All the awkwardness that had crept between her and Derek was gone. It had been as if they were a family today. Evelyn had forgotten what that was like. It was breaking her heart, knowing that this would probably be the only time she'd ever feel like she belonged.

You could change that.

She closed her eyes, trying to relax.

Tomorrow the fog would most likely lift and they would head back to Wolf's Harbor. Back to being doctors. And she would have to monitor Jennifer Yazzie like a hawk. She also knew she'd be on edge until those amnio results came in.

She opened her eyes and checked her phone, but there was nothing.

Dammit.

Mo giggled and Evelyn glanced at the television.

"What're you watching?"

"The Unicorn Princess," Mo said, not looking at her. "It's so funny. The unicorn is crazy."

"I can see," Evelyn said, and she *could* see, by the googly-eyed expression of the unicorn as it pranced after a very annoyed princess.

Mo yawned, and then to Evelyn's surprise curled up beside her.

"You smell nice, Evie. I like that," Mo said.

"You smell nice too," Evelyn whispered.

She reached down and tenderly ran her hand over Mo's curls. Mo snuggled in closer and it wasn't long before her laughter at the crazy antics of the unicorn disappeared and was replaced by a light snore.

Evelyn glanced down and saw that Mo was fast asleep, her head on her lap. Tears stung Evelyn's eyes and she stroked Mo's back.

Derek came out of the bathroom and his eyes widened in surprise. Then his expression softened as he looked at Mo.

"She's tired," Derek whispered, squatting down in front of them.

"She's not the only one." Evelyn smiled and then looked at Derek, whose eyes were sparkling the same way they had last night when they'd kissed.

She shivered as she recalled the way it had felt to be in his arms.

"I'll get her to bed," Derek said. He stood up and gently scooped Mo into his arms and carried her to the bedroom.

Evelyn shut off *The Unicorn Princess*.

Get control of yourself, Evelyn. He's off-limits.

Derek came out of the bedroom and shut the door. He headed for the kitchen and then produced a small bottle of wine.

"Where did you get that?" Evelyn asked.

"In the café when we got dinner. We have a nice little kitchen here, and I thought that after today, and you having to endure *The Unicorn Princess* while I showered, you could do with an adult beverage."

Evelyn chuckled. "Thanks. Yes, I definitely could."

Derek poured white wine into two tumblers and joined Evelyn on the couch. "Cheers, then."

Their glasses clinked and they both took a sip.

"Hey, I want to thank you for watching Mo. I rarely get a chance to be away from her and I

never have help…it was nice that she had someone else to focus on today."

"I don't mind. She's wonderful—tiring, but
wonderful."

Derek laughed softly. "Did you never want to
settle down and have kids? I mean, you mentioned not even picking another job."

"I never really thought about kids."

Liar.

"No serious relationships since Nathan?" he
asked.

She downed the rest of her wine. "No. Still not
ready."

Liar.

"Oh." Derek finished his own wine and settled
back against the couch.

"And what about you? How long has Mo's
mother been gone?"

"Five years."

"And?" Evelyn asked.

He shrugged. "I haven't had much time, what
with raising a baby on my own and my work…
My wife died during a snowstorm after giving
birth to Mo in our kitchen. Uterine rupture and
she bled out. There was nothing I could do to
save her. She died in my arms. By the time we

got her to Sitka she'd lost too much blood and she went into organ failure. And I was left with this tiny baby…this little girl…and I was alone." Derek clenched his fist. "I didn't get a chance to grieve. Mo was a newborn and I just had to keep going."

"I'm sorry."

And she was. Taking care of a practice and a newborn must've been hard. She'd watched her father for years doing the same and she'd been older. She was sympathetic.

"I understand," she said.

His expression softened to one of appreciation. "I know. You don't pity me and I appreciate it."

"Why would I pity you?"

"So many do." He sighed. "It's tiring."

"I admire you."

Their gazes locked and her cheeks flushed with warmth from the blush she was sure was there.

Derek cleared his throat. "This is why I fight constantly for a hospital—so other people don't have to feel the agony that I felt when I lost Vivian. When I wasn't a good enough doctor to save my own wife."

"It wasn't your fault, Derek. What happened to

Vivian was rare, but it happens. I'm sorry that it did. I understand."

"I appreciate you listening to me," he said. "No one seems to want to listen. They just offer condolences, pity, and move on."

"No problem," she said gently. "I'm here."

"Yeah and it's been nice."

Her pulse quickened. "Yes. It has been nice." *So nice.*

"It's not just that, though, that's been bothering me."

He took her glass and set it down. His eyes were intense again and she trembled as he moved closer to her.

"What else is bothering you?" she asked, blood thundering in her ears.

"It's wanting you. I want you, Evelyn, and even though I know you're leaving, and I shouldn't… I want you."

His admission caught her off guard, and made her head spin. "What…?"

"I have been numb for so long and you—you make me *feel* something again. Anger, frustration and yearning. Dammit, Evelyn, you're the most beautiful, stubborn, sexy woman who's walked into Wolf's Harbor in so long, and I've been trying to fight the urge to kiss you again."

The butterflies in her stomach were swirling around and her body burned with need. Something she'd never really felt before with any other man.

Don't let him in. Keep him at bay. You're leaving. You can't stay.

Only she didn't listen to that voice in her head. She wanted to feel as well. She'd been numb for so long too. Derek was the only man to evoke this kind of intense, burning desire in her and she wanted him too.

Even if it was for just one night.

She stood up and he touched her face, pushing back her hair before leaning down and kissing her.

Only this time there was no interruption. This time the light kiss which had ignited the flame when she'd first arrived burned hotter, deeper, as he pulled her tight against him, his arms around her as his tongue slipped past her lips, turning her legs to jelly.

She wanted to be close to him. Nothing between them. If she was going to have him only once she wanted to savor it, even if a part of her was telling her right now that once would never be enough.

She broke off the kiss, closing her eyes and reveling in the feeling of Derek's strong hands over her body.

"Don't stop," she whispered.

"I won't unless you want me to," Derek said against her ear, which caused a shiver of delight to course down her spine.

She wanted Derek to possess her.

His kisses trailed down from her ear to her neck and to her collarbone, his hands caressing her breasts under her scrub shirt.

"Too many clothes," Derek muttered.

"I can help with that."

Evelyn unbuttoned his shirt and ran her hands over his bare chest, then worked on his belt, pulling it out of the loops and snapping it as she tossed it over her shoulder. It caused his breath to hitch in his throat as she slipped her hands down the front of his jeans.

He slid his hand down her back and cupped her bottom. "You're taking too long," he moaned.

He pulled her close, kissing her, then pushed her away, pulling down his jeans so he was naked in front of her.

She ran her hands over him, felt his body stiffening under her touch.

"Your turn," he whispered.

She pulled off her shirt and shimmied out of her leggings. Derek stepped forward and removed her bra, leaving her in her pink cotton underwear.

"Beautiful," he murmured, sliding his hand down the front of her undies and stroking her. Making her moan in pleasure. Then he moved his hand and she took off her underwear, so she was standing there naked, exposed to him.

"You're blushing," he murmured, touching her cheek.

"It's been a while for me."

He smiled at her. "Me too."

He cupped her breast and the heat from his skin seared her flesh, making her body ache with need. Her body was so sensitive and she was completely lost to him. No man had ever had such control over her senses. It was scary and thrilling at the same time.

Derek scooped her up and carried her to the bed, pinning her to the mattress. Each time his fingers skimmed her flesh her body ignited. She wanted more from him. She wanted to catch fire and burn.

He stroked between her legs, making her wet with need, and her hips thrust up at him as he touched her.

"I need you, Evelyn."

"I want you too," she murmured. "There's a condom in my bag by the nightstand."

He rolled away and found the condom. She helped him put it on, stroking him.

Derek pressed her against the pillows and settled between her thighs, the tip of his erection pressing against her. He thrust into her quickly, filling her and making her cry out, cling to him.

"Did I hurt you?" he asked.

"No."

He made her feel like she'd never felt before.

"You feel so damn good."

Derek began to thrust and Evelyn urged him to go harder and faster. He unleashed something inside her. Something she'd never felt before. A coil of heat was unfurling in her, singeing her soul and possessing her.

Then it came—pleasure like she'd never had before. And she clung to Derek, crying out as she came. Derek quickened his pace and joined her, then held still over her, breathing heavily before slipping out of her and rolling to his side, his eyes closed.

Evelyn curled up next to him, felt his arm around her. They said nothing, because exhaustion had won over the euphoria, and as Evelyn drifted off to sleep she realized she was falling hard for Derek.

Heck, she'd already fallen hard for him.

She was angry at herself. He was vulnerable and she'd taken advantage of him. She was the worst. She didn't want a family because she didn't want to lose it. She knew that pain all too well.

But another part of her wanted it all. She was lonely and she was tired of running. She was tired of having no place to call home.

This could be your home?

She rolled on her side away from him.

She couldn't have it.

She couldn't risk it.

Why not?

And she rolled back to look at him, watching him sleep and recalling the way his lips had felt against hers, feeling the taste of him still branded there. She touched her lips, as if trying to imprint the feeling onto her fingertips.

Maybe she could stay?

There was nothing stopping her. Maybe, just maybe, she could be happy if she'd just take the chance.

CHAPTER ELEVEN

"I APPRECIATE YOU staying on, Tim," Derek said as he handed a file back to Dr. Vance.

They had gotten in late last night. And still all he could think about was what had happened in that cabin, the feeling that they were a family, and seeing Mo sleeping on Evelyn.

He couldn't help himself.

And even though he knew it shouldn't have happened, that night in the cabin had been wonderful. Amazing. It was hard not to think of the way her body had felt under his. The taste of her lips and the scent of her hair, the softness of her skin.

Focus.

He had to be careful.

He'd been lax in letting Evelyn in when he should've been guarding his heart. But it was difficult to do that around Evelyn. She got under all his defenses. But he couldn't let Mo get hurt.

She smells like coconut and tastes just as sweet.

He shook that thought out of his head.

"It's no problem, Derek," Tim replied. "I had some family stuff to attend to anyway. Besides, I enjoy my visits up here, and I wouldn't have given up the opportunity to watch Dr. Saunders in work."

Derek's stomach dropped as he saw the way that Tim was looking at Evelyn. Not that he could blame him in the least. Evelyn was beautiful, and a world-class doctor. Although Tim supposedly had a girlfriend in Sitka…

And even though he shouldn't let it bother him, because he had already made up his mind that he wasn't going to pursue Evelyn, he was jealous of another man looking at her. Because the simple fact of the matter was that he wished he was free to go after her. He wished she would stay. He wished he deserved her.

"It's not like I'll be doing much," Evelyn mumbled as she went through a chart at the front desk before the clinic opened, totally oblivious to Tim's interest in her.

Good.

"Still, Dr. Saunders, I would be keen to learn from you," Tim said eagerly.

Evelyn looked up. "Of course—and call me Evelyn. It's fine. We're all working together here. Now, if you'll both excuse me, I have to prep for a possible emergency C-section. We need to get a lot more blood stocked in the fridge here."

"Emergency C-section?" Tim asked, intrigued.

"Yes, one of my patients here has intrauterine growth restriction. She's on her way back from Juneau, where I performed an amniocentesis which I'm still waiting on results for. I have everything I need—including an incubator which was generously donated by Juneau General just in case."

"How nice of them," Derek teased and Evelyn grinned at him.

They both knew that it was a bribe to get her to consider working at Juneau when her time was up in Wolf's Harbor. Still, they weren't going to look a gift horse in the mouth.

"If I can help in any way, Evelyn. I'm here to assist you," Tim said eagerly. "I would *love* to assist you."

"I'm good for now—but, thanks." She wandered away, seemingly totally clueless about his compliments.

Derek chuckled to himself. She probably *wasn't* clueless to Tim's subtle flirting with her—she probably didn't care. And that was what he liked so much about her.

The phone rang and Tim answered it. "Wolf's Harbor Medical."

Evelyn blushed as Derek shared a look with her. They had both agreed in the morning that they wouldn't mention it anymore. That it had been just a weak moment. They would carry on as they always had. But still, watching her now in the clinic, being so close to her, it was hard not to think of her in his arms.

"How bad?" Tim asked, with an edge of concern in his voice.

Derek turned and watched as Tim took down information and then ended the call.

"What's wrong?" Derek asked.

"A young woman on the island up the channel—possible miscarriage and bleeding heavily." Tim handed the notes to Derek.

"Okay—you man the clinic and I'll get Evelyn out to Yashee Island."

"I can take Evelyn out to Yashee Island," Tim offered. "I would *love* to assist her."

Derek cocked any eyebrow. "Do you know where Yashee Island is? Do you have a boat?"

"Yes, I know where it is. I grew up here. But no boat."

"Then you stay here," Derek said.

Tim laughed. "I'm trying too hard, aren't I?"

"Just a bit. Stay here at the clinic and I'll get Evelyn out to the island."

"Okay, Derek." Tim chuckled.

Derek picked up his coat from the rack and went to exam room one, where Evelyn was preparing everything necessary for an emergency C-section.

"You're needed," Derek said.

She spun around. "Oh?"

"Possible miscarriage and heavy bleeding out on Yashee Island in the channel."

Evelyn frowned. "I'll get the gear ready. Is there a boat I can hire to take me out to the island?"

"I have a boat. Or rather the clinic has a boat for instances like this. I can take you and Tim will man the clinic."

"Great."

Evelyn went about packing everything she could need. She packed the Doppler, and Derek packed the cooler with some universal blood.

"Is there anything else we might need?" Derek

asked as he loaded the last of the gear into his car to take down to the docks.

"Well, if it's early on in her pregnancy a Doppler might not be able to pick up a heartbeat under ten weeks. An ultrasound would be best—but we can't transport that."

"No, we'd have to get her to the clinic for that."

"If she's hemorrhaging I'll need to get the bleeding to stop, but if it's a miscarriage I can usually tell in the pathology." She frowned. "This is the worst part of my specialty. Or one of the worst parts. We'll get the bleeding controlled and if the pregnancy is lost we'll get her back to the clinic to do an ultrasound and a dilation and curettage."

It was a short ride to the docks and they'd soon loaded and secured all the gear and headed out of the harbor toward the bay where Yashee Island lay, about five miles off the coast.

"It's really choppy today," Evelyn shouted over the roar of the engine.

"Storm is brewing somewhere. I'll check the radar tonight. It'll probably miss us. Good thing Joe and Jennifer are heading back right now. I would hate for them to be delayed or stuck somewhere."

"Well, if she was stuck in Juneau she'd be in good hands, but Joe texted me early this morning to say that they were catching the first ferry from Jordan Springs to Hoonah. They'll be here by dinnertime. What I'm waiting for is the results of that amnio."

Derek nodded. He could tell she was worried. He wanted to tell her it would be okay, but he was concerned too. He didn't say anything, though, because with the roar of the boat engine and the rough water, and the cold wind whipping up, the best course for Evelyn was to hunker down and keep warm.

It took him about twenty minutes to navigate the channel and then head out into the bay and deteriorating conditions towards Yashee Island. There were only about four families who lived on the small island, but all the homes were within walking distance of each other, and there were people waiting at the docks when they moored the boat there.

"Robert!" Derek called out as Robert Marshall, one of the island residents, helped him tie up his boat and bring the gear off.

"I got my ATV with a wagon loaded for your

gear. Saves lugging it over to the Washingtons' house."

Derek's stomach fell. "Martha?"

Robert nodded solemnly. "She came home from university about a month ago, pregnant, and this morning she woke up bleeding. Pretty bad too."

"This is Dr. Saunders, the OB/GYN currently on rotation in Wolf's Harbor."

Robert nodded curtly and then paused. "Thorne Saunders' girl?"

"Yes," Evelyn said, smiling. "Did you know him?"

"He was my doctor before…. A good man."

A strange expression passed over Robert's face as he helped carry the medical supplies up to his ATV. Derek couldn't help but wonder what that was all about.

He shook his head. He didn't have time to worry about it.

They secured the gear and then climbed into Robert's ATV. He drove them away from the docks, up the winding path to the house furthest from the landing: a log house high up the hill, hidden in the trees of Yashee Island. It boasted beautiful views.

The door opened and Derek saw Martha's mother Jocelyn standing there, waving.

"I'll bring up the rest of the gear, Docs. Go on and take care of your patient."

Robert handed Evelyn her medical bag and Derek led Evelyn up the path.

"So glad to see you, Dr. Taylor," Jocelyn said nervously. "I've been so worried. It hasn't stopped. The bleeding is so heavy."

"Well, thankfully our clinic has one of the best OB/GYNs from the eastern seaboard in service this month. Dr. Evelyn Saunders—this is Jocelyn Washington."

Jocelyn froze, her face paling, and Evelyn's mouth dropped open as they just stared at one another.

Derek was confused. They knew each other. Or it appeared that way.

Evelyn snapped her mouth shut and looked as if she was staring at a ghost. "I would like to see the patient now, if I could. If she's bleeding she needs medical attention."

"Of…of course. This way," Jocelyn said just as nervously as she led them into the house.

"You okay?" Derek asked.

"Leave it," Evelyn muttered under her breath

as she took off her boots and followed Jocelyn upstairs.

Derek stood there, still confused. It was apparent that Jocelyn and Evelyn knew each other, but the tension simmering under the surface was thick.

What was going on? What had happened?

Evelyn felt as if she was going to throw up. It had never occurred to her that she would run into Jocelyn again. She'd always been afraid of running into her. She'd ruined Jocelyn's life too.

It figured that just when Evelyn had found some sort of small happiness in Derek, karma had to remind her of what she'd done all those years ago.

Her father had wanted to marry Jocelyn. Jocelyn had wanted to replace her mother. And when she was a kid she'd hated Jocelyn. Now she had a hard time looking at her. Evelyn was ashamed of her past behavior.

"My daughter is in here," Jocelyn said quietly.

Evelyn barely acknowledged Jocelyn—because she couldn't look at her. She was having a hard time keeping her composure and she needed to have control. There was a young girl suffering and she needed help. She couldn't let her guilt over-power her and stop her from doing her job.

That was why she was here in Wolf's Harbor.

Evelyn walked into the room and saw a young girl of about nineteen on the bed, sweating. Her skin was gray and she knew just from the glassy expression in the young woman's eyes that she was bleeding and a lot of blood had been lost.

"Martha, I'm Dr. Saunders. I've come to help you."

Martha nodded, but clearly couldn't speak.

Evelyn pulled off her jacket and sanitized her hands. "Do you know how far along your daughter is, Mrs. Washington?"

"Sixteen weeks," Jocelyn answered, sitting next to her daughter.

"She's nineteen?" Evelyn asked.

"Yes," Jocelyn responded.

Well, it didn't take Jocelyn long to move on from my father.

She pushed that bitter thought away. At least Jocelyn had got some happiness. She deserved it.

"I'm going to examine you—okay, Martha? I'll take care of everything and then I'm going to have Dr. Taylor set up an IV for fluid and pain relief, okay?"

Martha nodded and closed her eyes.

Evelyn ignored the fact that Jocelyn was in the room. There was no time to think about that. She had to help this poor girl.

She had a job to do.

Evelyn came down the stairs, carrying her equipment. She was exhausted, but she'd managed to stop the bleeding. Now she just wanted to put some distance between her and Jocelyn.

There was so much she wanted to say to Jocelyn but couldn't. She was terrified. Terrified of having her apology rejected. She couldn't deal with that today.

Derek was waiting for her.

"Well?" he asked.

"Bleeding has slowed down and she's hooked up to some packed cells, but I need to get her into the clinic and do an ultrasound."

"Why?"

"I think she was pregnant with twins and she only lost one, because the Doppler picked up a heartbeat. I couldn't do anything else because I didn't want to jeopardize the baby, but she definitely miscarried just one. Her father has a boat and they're going to get her down to the docks.

We should get back to the clinic now and prepare for her arrival."

Derek nodded. "We can do that."

"Good." Evelyn slipped on her coat and then picked up a couple of boxes.

"Whoa, what's your rush?" Derek asked as he grabbed her by the arm and stopped her. "Aren't you going to say goodbye to Mrs. Washington?"

"I already have."

"You're so in a rush. Why?"

"I told you—we have to get the clinic ready." She walked out of the door.

Derek caught up to her as she made her way down the path toward the docks. "What're you running from?"

"I'm not running from anything."

Liar.

"Oh, come on, Evelyn, you were positively rude to Jocelyn Washington and you've never, not once, been rude to *anyone* in town."

Evelyn glared at him. "Derek, if the other twin is currently alive I have to prepare everything back at the clinic to make sure it stays that way. Martha was absolutely devastated that she lost one. I promised her and her mother I would do everything in my power to save the other twin.

I'm not running from anything. Honestly? I'm still a bit tired from our trip to Juneau."

"Fine," Derek said, but she could tell from his tone that he wasn't fine.

Evelyn was relieved when he dropped it. He didn't need to know that Jocelyn had been going to marry her father. Or that her father had been killed on his way to visit her. Part of her felt guilty about the whole thing, because her father had gone out that night to propose and he'd died. But the adult version of her wanted to know more.

Her gut reaction to Jocelyn had been cold. Now she was ashamed with herself for her behavior. Would Jocelyn have said yes? Jocelyn had lost someone that night too.

They loaded the boat and headed back to Wolf's Harbor. There was a fog over the water so thick it was hard to see, and she hoped that Martha's family would be able to get her into the clinic.

Derek wasn't saying anything to her and that was for the best.

She really didn't want to talk about it.

When they got back to the clinic Evelyn dried off and got the exam room ready, prepping the ultrasound with Janet.

Thirty minutes later Martha Washington was

brought in on a stretcher by the paramedics, who had been called and had been waiting for the Washingtons' boat when it moored at the town's docks.

Jocelyn followed Martha in, but didn't look at Evelyn.

Evelyn couldn't blame her. She was so embarrassed over her behavior. She'd acted badly. She deserved Jocelyn's cold shoulder.

They got Martha transferred to the exam table, and when the paramedics had left Evelyn examined Martha. The bleeding had subsided.

"Give her another unit of packed cells, Janet," Evelyn said as she covered Martha up and wheeled the ultrasound machine over.

"She's stopped bleeding?" Jocelyn asked.

Evelyn met Jocelyn's gaze and nodded. "Yes, you can see for yourself. Her color is returning to normal. Martha, how is your pain?"

"It's a five now, Dr. Saunders."

Evelyn smiled warmly. "Better than the ten it was before. I know your belly is tender, but I'm going to do an ultrasound. I heard a heartbeat on the Doppler and I want to confirm that you were indeed carrying twins and that the other twin is fine."

Martha nodded.

Evelyn got the gel ready. "It'll be cold... Here we go. Janet, can you get the lights?"

"Yes, Dr. Saunders."

Janet dimmed the lights and Evelyn placed the wand on Martha's belly. She soon found what she was looking for. There was the strong flutter of a heartbeat for the other twin. She grinned and turned the monitor.

"There you go, Martha. You *were* pregnant with twins. You lost one, but this one right here has a strong heartbeat."

Martha began to cry, and Jocelyn bent down and kissed her daughter on the head.

"Now what, Dr. Saunders?" Martha asked nervously. "I don't want to lose my other baby."

"Bed-rest, and I'll want to check on the baby tomorrow, so you guys should stay here for the night. I want to monitor your bleeding and do another ultrasound before you head back to the island. You'll have to come in for regular check-ups for a while."

"Can she do that on bed-rest?" Jocelyn asked.

"Yes, but she needs to take it easy and rest wherever possible."

"We can stay in town, Mom, at our old house."

Jocelyn bit her lip and then smiled nervously as she glanced at Evelyn. "Yes. Of course."

"Well, it's good you kept two residences."

"Well, Mom didn't marry my stepdad until I was ten. My real father was killed in an accident before I was born. In fact, come to think of it, we have the same last name, Dr. Saunders."

Jocelyn's eyes were wide with fear as Evelyn's world teetered out of control. And as she looked at Martha for the first time—*really* looked at Martha—she saw her father's eyes. Saw her father's ruddy hair and freckles.

Evelyn favored her mother, and had missed out on her father's freckles, but she'd inherited his hair. Except hers was auburn—red mixed with her mother's dark. Martha looked like pictures of her late grandmother when she was young.

This was her half sister.

Oh, God. I ruined this girl's life too.

She had to get out of here.

"Well, it's a common surname. Now, I have to check on something—Janet will make sure you're comfortable."

Evelyn peeled off her rubber gloves and disposed of them as she quickly left the room.

Jocelyn followed her. "Evelyn, wait!"

Evelyn spun around. "No. We're not talking about it."

"I think we *should* talk."

Evelyn was shaking—with anger, pain, and just about every raw emotion she could think of. She didn't know what to think. What to believe. Everything inside her was telling her to run, which would save her from getting hurt.

"No. I can't… I can't talk about it now. I'm sorry."

She grabbed her coat and walked out of the clinic and straight into the rain. She wandered along the main street, not really knowing where she was going.

Her mind was screaming at her, telling her to pack a bag and leave.

She needed to protect her heart. When her father had died and she'd lost her home and the only family she'd ever known she'd sworn to herself that she would never feel that kind of pain again.

She didn't want a family. Families got shattered, broken, and people ended up alone.

You have one, though. Why can't you see that?

Evelyn continued wandering until she was standing in front of a clapboard house that had used to be bright red, but was now faded and chipped. Everything was the same—including the covered porch with the rocking chair. Only no one was home. The lights were out. The car was gone...

"Evelyn?" Derek said in confusion. "You're soaked."

Evelyn turned. "How did you find me?"

"I had a hunch."

"Good hunch." She chuckled nervously.

"Come on—my car is over here. I'll take you back to your place."

He slipped his arm around her and led her the way to his car and out of the rain.

It was comforting.

It felt good that someone cared for her.

They didn't say much as he drove her back to the clinic and led her to the apartment in the back. Once they were inside he took off her coat.

"Go get changed and I'll make some tea."

Evelyn nodded and went to change into dry clothes. By the time she was done the tea was ready.

"Thank you, Derek," she said, not knowing what else to say. She was appreciative of the fact that he'd found her standing in the rain before anyone else had seen her.

He nodded. "What would you like in your tea? Honey or lemon?"

"Something stronger?" she said dryly.

Derek laughed and pulled out some whiskey. "This do?"

"Yes!"

Derek poured them both tea with a shot of whiskey. "Do you want to talk about it?"

"No," she muttered. "Not really."

"Okay."

She scrubbed a hand over her face, because she needed to talk about it to *someone*.

"Martha Washington is my half sister."

His eyes widened briefly. "Oh. That I didn't know."

"That's all I'll say."

"Okay," he said.

"I know you think I have walls..."

"I told you—we all have walls, Evie. I'm just glad that you've decided to let me in."

Tears stung Evelyn's eyes. "What am I doing here?"

"You've come home to lay some ghosts to rest.

It's obvious." Derek finished his tea. "And to practice medicine, obviously?"

"You think so?" she teased, and then sighed.

"Well, you *are* a doctor." He winked.

Evelyn laughed, felt her mood lifting.

"If I had just accepted that my father wanted to marry again I could've had a sister. I wouldn't have had to leave."

Derek sighed. "We can't look at the past. It's hard, but we just have to do what's right going forward."

She nodded. "I suppose you're right."

"I know I am. Now, I'm going to head back down to the clinic. I'll see you later."

He pulled her close into a warm hug and she tried not to cling to him, but it felt so good to be in his arms.

After he'd left her phone buzzed and she picked it up. It was an email from Juneau General Hospital and her heart skipped a beat.

It was Jennifer's results.

She had to get to her computer and analyze them.

She was hoping the baby didn't have any chromosomal defects. She was hoping the baby would be able to survive an emergency birth if it came

down to it. But if the baby had issues she was
going to put Jennifer on a plane to Sitka and deliver the child.

Then, when Martha was stable and Jennifer's
baby was safe, she was going to get the heck out
of Wolf's Harbor.

She'd done her duty to her father. She was tired
of ghosts.

Forgive yourself.

Only she couldn't. She'd caused too much pain
and she had to leave before she caused anymore.

And the only way she'd escape was if she ran—
and that was what she planned to do as soon as
she could.

CHAPTER TWELVE

"WHAT DO YOU MEAN, a hurricane is tracking toward us?" Derek asked.

Tim Vance showed him the emergency report that was flashing on his laptop. "It's rare, but a hurricane that cropped up off the coast of Hawaii is building strength and heading straight for us. They're warning all residents of southeast Alaska to brace for hurricane conditions."

"Is Juneau included?"

Tim nodded.

Derek's heart skipped a beat and he picked up the phone to call his in-laws. He owed Vivian that much.

"Hi, George, it's Derek. Yeah, Mo is okay... But have you and Melanie heard about the hurricane? Okay, good. Stay safe. I know. Thanks."

Derek ended the call. His in-laws had already heard about the hurricane barreling its way toward them and had taken precautions, boarding up their windows and stocking their house with supplies. And they'd reminded him to take care of Mo more than once. He knew they blamed him for Vivian's death, because they'd told him so—many times.

Mo would be okay with Edna at the house until he was able to get out there and collect her. It would be best if they all just hung out at the clinic until it blew over. And he was positive that Evelyn would let them crash at her place.

"Do you know when it's supposed to hit?" Derek asked Tim.

"Tonight."

"I think we're going to stay here tonight, then. We have Martha still resting until Dr. Saunders discharges her. I'll have to go get Mo and bring her in here."

"I'll get her," Janet offered. "I have to check on my place and it's on the way."

"Are you sure, Janet? Edna is with her—do you think you can bring Edna back into town too?"

"Yeah, of course. I've watched Mo before, and I know she likes riding in my truck, and picking up Edna is no problem." Janet grabbed her coat. "I'll get your house locked up too, and get some supplies."

"Thanks, Janet. And if you see Dr. Saunders tell her I need her."

Janet nodded and left just as Evelyn walked in. There were dark circles under her eyes. She looked exhausted.

"What happened to you?" Derek asked.

"I got the results in from Jennifer's amnio. I spent all last night analyzing them." She scrubbed a hand over her face. "How's Martha?"

"Stable," Tim answered. "I just went to check on her. They're wondering when they can leave. Mrs. Washington wants to get their home stocked up before the hurricane hits."

Evelyn's eyes widened. "Hurricane?"

"Yeah—they're grounding all planes," Derek said.

"Right. Well, I just went to check on Jennifer Yazzie. Baby is strong and no signs of labor. Let's hope it stays that way until the planes have clearance to fly, and then I'm getting her to Sitka as soon as possible."

"Why? Is it bad?" Derek asked.

"No chromosomal abnormalities, but Jennifer has symptoms of the beginning stages of kidney failure and the baby has polycythemia."

"What's that?" Tim asked.

"A concentration of red blood cells," Derek answered. "Not fatal, but it can cause complications."

"I need to get that baby out of her." Evelyn hung up her jacket. "I'll go check on Martha and get her discharged."

Derek nodded. "Okay, and then we need to get this clinic ready for the hurricane."

She nodded and disappeared into the back room.

In all his fifteen years in Alaska he'd never encountered a hurricane. They were rare in Alaska, but not unheard of. Hopefully this hurricane would lose steam, or the jet stream would make it change direction so they didn't get slammed with one.

Alaska got storms, even tropical ones, and really bad winter storms, but this was the first time a hurricane was coming to batter his clinic.

"Nancy?" Derek called out to his receptionist, who was in the filing cabinet. "Do we have any protocols for hurricanes?"

"Yes, Dr. Taylor." Nancy went over to a drawer and pulled out a binder. "Every possible natural disaster is listed in there."

"Great—and now you're going home."

"Dr. Taylor, I can stay and help."

"No, Nancy. You go home. You've got kids, and you need to make sure your house is ready for this storm. Go—and that's an order. I would send Janet too, but we're going to need her once she gets back."

"Thank you, Dr. Taylor." Nancy collected up her things and left.

Derek sat down behind her desk with the binder and flipped to the page about hurricanes. They could hole up in here. After Evelyn had taken care of Martha and sent her on her way they'd raid Evelyn's apartment for food and supplies and then board up her windows before securing the clinic.

At least they had enough supplies. At least people could get to them for help. Unlike the night that big snow storm had hit and he'd lost his Vivian because she hadn't been able to get the emergency care she'd needed.

"We were called for a transfer?" said Dan, one of the paramedics, from the door.

Evelyn came out. "Yes, Martha Washington. You have the address. But she needs to lie flat for a bit longer."

Dan nodded and they followed her in with a stretcher.

It wasn't long before they were bringing Martha out. She didn't have an IV anymore and looked better.

"Don't try to come out if there's a hurricane. When it's all clear drive her over to the clinic and I'll do an ultrasound," Evelyn warned.

"Thank you, Dr. Saunders," Jocelyn said, not looking at her.

When Martha was loaded into the ambulance Evelyn came back inside.

"Okay, what do we have to do to get ready for this hurricane?"

"Supplies. Food and water. All of us are going to crash here tonight. I'm going to drive out to my place and secure it, also grab as much bottled water and food as I can, and Tim will help you with your apartment."

"Okay."

"Planes are grounded, as you know, and ferry service has stopped. All the roads out of town are closed except for emergency services. It's a complete shut-down."

"Yeah, we used to have hurricanes in Boston.

I remember. I'll take what I can and we'll meet back here in a couple of hours."

"Sounds good."

Janet called to say she was delayed. The wind had picked up and there were trees that had been knocked over, blocking the road back into town.

Edna, Mo and Janet were at Janet's place while the trees were cleared by the volunteer fire department.

Derek was stressed, but he knew Mo was safe with Edna and Janet, so he focused on battening down the hatches at the clinic. They would need the generator when the power went out, so he took stock of the supplies he could grab and other essential items—including another generator.

Lives depended on those generators.

By the time he'd finished unloading everything into the storeroom Evelyn and Tim were bringing down boxes of food from her place.

The apartment was on higher ground, but it had more windows. The clinic didn't have as many interior windows and they would be safer there. He was glad that the clinic was high above the sea walls that surrounded the lower part of town and the downs. They were perfectly situated on the hill.

It was then that the rain hit. And it was heavy.

"What time is this hurricane coming?" Derek asked.

"I'll check the weather network." Tim pulled out his phone. "Two hours it'll make landfall. It's large. So when it makes landfall in Sitka it's going to hit us."

"This clinic has back-up generators, right?" Evelyn asked worriedly.

"Of course. We'll be fine. You seem agitated? I thought you were used to hurricanes."

"I have a bad feeling," she muttered, and she was twitching nervously.

Derek wanted to comfort her, but not in front of Tim. Besides, he was worried about Mo and hoped the road would be cleared soon.

He had to keep his distance from her. That was what they'd agreed upon. It was for the best. If he comforted her now, he wouldn't be able to stop himself. She'd draw him in again. Get through his defenses.

Who are you kidding? She already had. Evelyn had a way about her that just drew him in and he was a lost man.

"Where's Janet? I thought she'd be back with Mo," Evelyn asked, and there was concern in her voice.

"Tree fell, blocking the road. They'll be here as soon as it clears."

Evelyn still looked worried and it melted his heart, seeing her concern for his daughter.

She loved Mo too. It was obvious.

He wrapped his arm around her and gave her a hug. She rested her head on his shoulder. It was comforting, sharing this burden with someone else, with her. He didn't feel so alone.

Only you are.

He broke the connection.

"Come on—let's finish boarding up the windows of the clinic," Derek said.

They worked together in uneasy silence. Then Derek made a preliminary check on the generators. Outside it was growing dark, which was unusual it being summer time in Alaska.

It was eerie. He could hear the rain pelting the metal roof and the sides of the clinic. It was harder than it had been before. Once that gale force wind picked up it wouldn't be safe for anyone out there on the street.

What was that old saying? It wasn't that the

wind was blowing, but what the wind was blowing around? He glanced at the clock.

How long did it take to clear a tree from a road anyway?

"Help!"

Derek ran from the back as he saw Joe Jr. come in, supporting Jennifer. On her other side was Joe Sr.

Evelyn came rushing from the back room. "Jennifer!"

Jennifer was moaning in pain, doubled over, and Derek's chest tightened as he saw himself in Joe's shoes, holding Vivian as she cried out.

"She went into labor, Evie," Joe Jr. said. "It happened so fast. One minute she was fine and the next her water broke."

"Her water broke? Get her into exam room one," Evelyn said.

She was cursing under her breath as Joe Jr. scooped up his wife and carried her to the back.

Joe Sr. and Tim braced the door shut, locking it as the wind hit, trying to throw it open with a god-awful howl which made Derek's insides turn into ice. It reminded him of the night Mo was born. The storm that had hit then. The howl and groan of the wind as it had dumped snow, almost burying them alive and impeding the medical attention Vivian had needed. They hadn't been able to get out and by the time help came it had been too late.

That storm had cost Vivian her life, and he prayed that this storm wouldn't cost Jennifer hers.

Derek headed to the back room and helped Joe lie Jennifer on the operating table. Evelyn was in the next room, putting on scrubs. He could see the look of dread on her face as she did so.

Tim was prepping Jennifer, and was already in a set of scrubs. Jennifer was unconscious, the pain having overtaken her.

"What's going to happen, Dr. Taylor?" Joe asked with terror in his eyes. "I can't lose her!"

"Come on, Joe. Let's go sit with your dad. Let Evie take care of her."

Tim ran past him to lend a hand as Derek walked Joe Jr. back to his father.

"What do we do?" Joe Sr. asked.

"I have to go help, but Jennifer is in safe hands, Joe. Evie is a good doctor. A good surgeon. Evelyn is brilliant."

And he would be there, every step of the way.

It wasn't ideal, but they wouldn't lose Jennifer or the baby.

He had every confidence.

This time he would win out over death.

"It will be fine, Joe."

Joe nodded nervously and didn't respond, but Derek had a good feeling that Evelyn would save Jennifer's life.

He was willing to bet on it.

Evelyn gave him hope even though he was worried about the storm, about Mo—about a lot. The one thing he was sure of, that he believed in, was Evelyn.

She'd done it before and he knew she'd do it again.

She might have a complicated past, like him, but she didn't let it interfere with her work.

The past was in the past. That was what he'd told her the other day when she'd opened up about Martha.

He had never thought he'd say that.

Ever.

But he'd meant it. Evelyn had given him hope for so much more. If he could just let go…

"I know anesthetics," Tim said as he finished scrubbing and headed into exam room one, which was now an operating theater. "I can manage her airway."

"Great," Evelyn said as she got into a surgical gown and gloves. "We'll deliver this baby here and now. Tim, get the incubator ready when Jennifer's anesthesia is stable."

"Of course, Dr. Saunders."

Derek came into the scrub room and changed in front of her. She was grateful that he was going to assist. She needed Janet to manage the baby while Evelyn operated on Jennifer and got her stable. Then Evelyn could focus on keeping the baby alive.

"There was meconium in the water," Evelyn said to Derek as he finished scrubbing and got a gown on.

"That's bad," Derek said.

"Yeah, I'm worried the baby aspirated it, and that's a definite sign of distress. The baby's heart-rate is elevated. We need to get that baby out of there."

The wind howled and the clinic creaked. The lights flickered and Evelyn took a deep breath.

You got this. You can do this.

"Back-up generators are running. If we lose main power we have the back-ups, and the incubator has a battery pack that is charged." Derek smiled from behind his surgical mask. "I'm glad you're here."

"Thanks." She sighed. "Let's go."

Evelyn took a deep breath as she entered the makeshift operating room. She wasn't used to conditions like this. She was used to state-of-the-art facilities. Large operating theaters that were fully staffed, and a gallery full of eager interns and residents who wanted to learn.

She wasn't used to working in the wilds of Alaska, where situations like this meant life or death.

The lights flickered again, but came back on. *Just stay on. Please.*

This was what her father had done every day. There had been no specialists flying in. It had just been him.

She could do this because she had Derek by her side. Because this baby and Jennifer were family. She had to make sure she didn't lose any more family members.

She'd ruined enough lives.

She took her spot and went to work. She washed Jennifer's abdomen with betadine and then picked a scalpel off the tray. She drowned out the sounds of the storm, of the monitors, and of everything else.

The only sound she focused on was her heart. The only voice she heard in her head was her own, telling her what move to make.

She'd done countless C-sections before.

This was no different.

Evelyn looked up and saw Derek across from her, holding the retractor. He nodded and she reached in and pulled out a tiny thirty-three-week-old baby boy. He wasn't breathing, but that was to be expected. She was prepared for that.

She quickly cut the cord and handed the baby over to Tim, who was holding out towels. Tim whisked him over to the warming table and there was a tiny cry, but it wasn't strong.

Still, it was a cry, and tears stung her eyes as she thought of her little third cousin—alive.

Family.

"Keep him ventilated, Tim—and warm."

"Yes, Dr. Saunders."

Evelyn finished her work on Jennifer and made sure she was stable. She closed her up and injected antibiotics into her IV. Jennifer was going to make it.

Thank goodness.

She wanted to cry for joy, but she kept her emotions in check.

"Take her into the other exam room, Derek—and, Tim, bring her out of the anesthetic."

Tim nodded, but Derek stayed by the incubator.

"Is something wrong, Derek?" Evelyn asked.

"Nothing. He's breathing with the vent and his stats are good."

Thank God.

"Good. That's good. And Jennifer will survive."

And that was the only answer she could give. It was a relief.

"The baby will need the services of a neonatal doctor. I hope this storm lets up soon. I'm going to stay here with him now."

"Dr. Saunders!" Tim shouted. "There's blood in the drainage tube of the IV line."

Evelyn whipped back around.

Oh, God.

"I need to open her up again. I think her uterus has ruptured. Hang blood. Lots of blood."

And she was glad the stock of blood she ordered, for this reason, had come in before the planes had all been grounded.

Evelyn quickly worked on getting back in there to try and fix the damage.

Derek was pale as he stepped back. "What's happening?"

"She's bleeding out. I need help, Derek!"

"Tell me what to do!" Derek said, jumping back into the fray with her.

Evelyn knew this was hard for him after what had happened to his wife, but she also knew he was strong. Stronger than he gave himself credit for. Stronger than her. He was there, by her side, ready to save a life. He was a doctor first and foremost, and a damn fine one that she could rely on.

The first man in a long time she could rely on.

Even though Mo was still out in that storm he didn't fold under pressure. And she wouldn't either. He gave her strength in this moment. Strength she hadn't thought she had.

And she was glad he was here.

With him she couldn't fail.

She *wouldn't* fail.

CHAPTER THIRTEEN

HURRICANE TINA LASTED for twelve hours before it moved over the mainland and lost steam.
The tree on the road was cleared. Janet, Mo and
Edna made it safely to the clinic. There was no
way Edna could get home yet, but her family was
safe and everyone was relieved that the three of
them were okay. Derek had Mo resting in his office and Edna had taken one of the empty exam
rooms.

Evelyn was exhausted. She'd managed to stop
Jennifer's bleeding, but Jennifer would need a
hysterectomy. They had to get her into Sitka.

The baby was still alive and she'd given him
some saline and packed cells to try and dilute the
packed red blood cells. His lungs were wet and
underdeveloped still, even though Jennifer had
been given a shot of steroids in Juneau to help
quicken lung development.

Little Baby Boy Yazzie still had a long way

to go. He needed to be in a neonatal intensive care unit.

Jennifer was still under sedation because of her blood loss and the major surgery.

Evelyn and Janet traded on watching the baby in the incubator. Just so they could have a break to stretch or eat or have coffee.

Evelyn's eyelids felt as if they were made of sandpaper now, as she sat next to the incubator, monitoring the tiny little infant.

Her third cousin was cute.

Evelyn smiled at him. She might have told herself she never wanted to have a family, or planned on it because she was too terrified, but she really did want one. A husband, kids, and to travel around the world.

That would be perfection.

Or you could just stay here.

"The planes are back up and running," Tim announced as he came in from the staff room. "The hurricane is over, just a tropical storm now, and the air ambulance is ready to take Jennifer and Joe the Third to Sitka."

Evelyn raised her eyebrows. "Joe the Third?"

Tim laughed and left the room.

She turned back to the baby. "Sorry, kid. I mean sorry about being Joe the Third."

Evelyn stood up, her body aching from being hunched over. She grabbed the chart she'd been keeping and stuck it under the incubator. The paramedics were already wheeling Jennifer out and Joe Jr. looked beside himself.

"She's not awake," he said when he saw Evelyn.

"I've kept her out—she's been through a lot. She'll wake up soon. She's stable, Joe. Remember? We talked about it? She'll need you when she wakes up."

Joe nodded and then looked at the incubator. Evelyn hadn't let him get too close to Joe the Third because she didn't want to put any strain on the baby.

Joe Jr. grinned and Joe Sr. came over.

"He'll be fine too," Evelyn said. "He needs to spend time in the neonatal intensive care unit, but he's made it this long."

"Thank you, Evie," said Joe Jr., and followed the paramedics outside with Jennifer.

Joe Sr. lingered behind and looked at his grandson. "Your parents would be so proud, Evelyn. If it wasn't for you I don't think Jennifer or the baby would be here. Thank you."

Evelyn nodded, but she didn't know how to respond to that at all. She wheeled Joe the Third out to the ambulance and the incubator was loaded in beside Jennifer and Joe Jr.

She stood there watching as they secured them and then shut the doors. The ambulance fired up and headed toward the airport, where the air ambulance was waiting to take them to Sitka.

Evelyn walked slowly back into the clinic.

She was wiped out.

"Have you seen Derek, Tim?"

Tim stretched where he was sitting behind the reception desk. "No, not since the surgeries."

Evelyn frowned. "I'm going to have a shower. Think you can man things here?"

Tim nodded. "I'm fine. I'll clean up and then lock up."

"Send Janet and Edna home too. It's been a long day and night. I'm sure they want to get home to check on their families."

Tim nodded. "Of course. Get some rest."

"You too."

Evelyn grabbed her coat and headed outside. There were a few fallen branches and some garbage littering the street. The damage wasn't bad. there was some flooding near the sea wall, and it might take some time to clear that, only she wouldn't be here to see it.

She couldn't stay here anymore.

Why not?

Evelyn cursed under her breath, annoyed at herself.

Being with Derek had been amazing, but what would he think of her if he knew the truth about her.

She'd ruined so many lives and now she was too hardened. Her grandmother had taught her well.

What if she ruined his life too? Or Mo's?

Derek and Mo deserved more than her. It had been a mistake coming here. She should've just turned down her friend's plea for help. Coming to Alaska had been a bad idea.

Had it, though?

Derek had dozed off with Mo. She'd been terrified of being separated from him, and when he'd got her settled down he hadn't been able to help drifting off.

He didn't sleep long before he woke with a start and remembered in crystal clarity everything that had happened. He reached over for Mo, worried that he'd lost her, but she was there.

Where was Evelyn?

And then he remembered Jennifer Yazzie.

He scrubbed his hands over his face, feeling emotionally drained because what had happened with Jennifer had reminded him of what he'd gone through with Vivian. Only for a moment, though. Jennifer was here still. The baby was stable. Strong. This was not a tragedy all because of Evelyn. She had brought light to the darkness.

Derek groaned and got up. He was angry at himself for sleeping with Evelyn, for giving in to the desire that he knew was wrong, but it had been worth it.

And, though he should feel worse than he did, he had loved being with Evelyn that way. He'd loved taking her in his arms. It had felt so natural to be with her and it had been so long since a woman had made him feel that way.

Evelyn made him *feel* again.

He wasn't Dr. Taylor and he wasn't Mo's dad when he was in her arms.

He was a hot-blooded man again.

What about Vivian?

Derek was confused about his feelings. All he

knew right now, in this moment, was that one night with Evelyn would never be enough.

Maybe, just maybe, he could give this a shot?

He'd never thought he'd find anyone again after Vivian had died. He'd never thought he'd see hope in hopeless situations. He'd never thought he'd feel alive again, but Evelyn had changed that.

He was in love with Evelyn. He'd fallen in love with her.

He just wasn't sure if Evelyn reciprocated those feelings.

She was holding back. She was hiding something. And until she opened up he wasn't sure she'd let him in. And he had to protect Mo from getting hurt.

He got himself and Mo up and dressed and then drove to drop Mo at Edna's. As he walked back towards the front of the clinic he saw a person crossing the road. Before he could figure out who it was the person collapsed in a heap.

"Oh, my God!"

Derek ran over and saw it was Jocelyn Washington. She was unconscious.

"Hold on, Jocelyn!" He assessed her ABCs and

saw there was a laceration to her head that was bleeding.

Tim ran out of the clinic, having been watching from the window. "What happened?"

"Jocelyn fainted. We need a backboard. Help Evelyn bring one out."

Tim nodded and ran off. Evelyn came outside within a few minutes, carrying a backboard with Tim.

"Great," Derek said.

"I saw the whole thing happen." Evelyn looked down at Jocelyn and paused. "She just collapsed."

"She's okay. I don't think she hit her head too hard. Now, *why* she fainted is another matter."

"This street is where my father died," she muttered as she helped Derek assess Jocelyn and then together they lifted her onto the backboard and carried her into the clinic.

"This is not your father, Evelyn. Jocelyn was not hit by a car."

Evelyn nodded and they carried Jocelyn into an exam room.

Jocelyn was coming to, groaning in pain.

"Jocelyn—it's Dr. Taylor. You fainted in the street and hit your head pretty bad."

Jocelyn didn't respond and Derek checked her pupils. They were reactive.

"She probably has a concussion," Evelyn said.

Tim came in and Evelyn stepped back, because Tim had more training in emergency medicine than she did.

"Abdomen is soft."

Jocelyn came around. "What happened?"

"You fainted in the street."

"Oh, my God." She tried to sit up.

"Don't move, Jocelyn. You hit your head hard and probably have a concussion. Lie still. We're going to get you taken care of."

Jocelyn nodded. She was in shock.

"Evelyn?" Jocelyn whispered.

Evelyn nodded, but Jocelyn still appeared stunned.

"Evelyn!" Jocelyn shouted as she stared at her with a dazed expression.

"Yes?" Evelyn said.

"I loved your father."

"I know," she said.

"He loved you more. That night he was distracted because you were upset about us. He wanted to get back to you and he didn't pay attention crossing the road. The ring he bought me—I had to sell it because I was alone and pregnant after he died. *You* were more important to him. It was *your* fault. *All* of it."

"Hey, now," Derek said to Jocelyn. "You need to stop talking."

Evelyn's cheeks were flushed with embarrassment as she left the exam room.

Jocelyn settled down and drifted off. Definitely a concussion.

"You got this, Tim?" Derek asked. "I'm going to call Jocelyn's family and let them know where she is."

Tim nodded. "Yep. I got this."

Derek left the room and found Evelyn in the storeroom, pacing.

"Hey, what she said…she has a concussion."

"I know, but it's got a lot of truth to it," Evelyn said. "I didn't know he'd asked her to marry him. But I knew he wanted to, and I was upset that night he left. I've blamed myself for so long for his death. I didn't realize she blamed me as well."

"I'm sorry."

Evelyn shrugged. "Well, it's not going to bring my father back."

"No."

She sighed. "I called Juneau General and they're

going to send a replacement OB/GYN out here to finish off my rotation."

Derek was stunned. "What?"

"I have to go," Evelyn said quickly. "I can't stay here."

"You can finish out your rotation."

"No, I can't. I have to get out of here. I can't live in the past. I have to move on. I have to forget about this place. I've done too much damage."

"What're you talking about?"

Evelyn sighed. "I told you that Martha Washington is my half sister. Because of me not wanting my dad to marry Jocelyn he was killed that night. It was always bad enough that I ruined two lives—but three? I have to leave before I hurt them further."

"What?" Derek was in shock, blocking her escape from the storeroom. "You're leaving?"

"I can't stay."

"Why? What about your family here?"

"What *about* them? They got along fine without me for twenty years."

"That's because your grandmother blocked them."

"My grandmother was grieving for her son."

"Evelyn, Wolf's Harbor needs you. I—" Only

he couldn't finish that sentence. He couldn't finish what he wanted to say.

What about me? What about Mo?

"I can't stay. I can't deal with this. It's twenty years too late to mourn. I've got a good life and I have to put this place behind me. I can't..."

"You're afraid. You couldn't settle down with a man you'd been with for two years and you can't take a chance with your heart now."

"I'll ruin your life if I stay. I'm too hardened. I don't have the room or the capacity," she said stonily.

"You improved my life. You lit up this town. You have to stay."

"What's two more months going to do? Nothing will change."

The question caught him off guard and he realized that she'd never been going to stay. She'd never planned on staying.

"I *knew* it was a mistake. I knew it was a mistake getting close to you. I *told* myself that you weren't going to stay. You temporary doctors create more problems than you fix, coming through here."

"There was always a time limit on this, Derek. I can't stay any longer. Besides, if Mo changed her mind about sharing her father... Don't do what my father did to me. Don't do that to Mo."

Derek couldn't look at her. His heart was breaking but he couldn't figure out why. How could a heart love two people at once?

"Well," he said calmly, "you better get packed up. I'll check on your half sister."

"She's not my family, Derek. I lost my family a long time ago."

"No, you didn't lose them. They're right here. You're just too scared to find them again."

Evelyn's gaze narrowed. "I'm not the only one scared here, Derek. You're just as afraid of forgiveness as I am. You can't forgive yourself for Vivian, just like me and my father's death."

He stepped to the side and let her leave.

She slammed the door behind her and Derek kicked the wall.

Uncle Yazzie drove her to the airport. He'd been surprised when she called, but he'd come just the same.

He didn't say anything to her as he drove her away from the clinic.

Always running.

As she looked back at the clinic through the

window she realized that she was tired of running, but she'd ruined more lives here than she'd saved.

That's not true.

Derek's words about her lighting up Wolf's Harbor resonated with her.

She was so hardened, like her grandmother. Her grandmother had been miserable and bitter all the years Evelyn had known her. But she could've been happy had she just accepted Thorne's life in Alaska. Her grandmother had deprived herself of happiness and Evelyn was doing the same.

She stared down at the box and the card on her lap that Uncle Yazzie had given to her from Léelk'w. Evelyn couldn't bring herself to open it.

"Are you sure about this, Evie?" Uncle Yazzie asked from the front seat.

No.

"Yes."

"This is your home." He parked the cab and turned around. "Don't leave. Stay. This is where you belong."

"I don't belong here, Uncle Yazzie. I did once, but..." There were so many pieces of her life that were missing. So much she'd missed out on. So much she'd lost.

She'd hardened her heart for so long that she wasn't sure that she could go back.

Ever.

"I think I'm going to take a job I've been offered in Seattle. I'll come to visit," Evelyn said, but they both knew that was a lie.

"You don't think that you fit in here, but you do, Evie. I just wish you could see that." He climbed out of the cab and went to the trunk to get her bags.

Evelyn slipped out of the cab and took the bags from him. He hugged her and Evelyn closed her eyes, fighting tears.

Keep it together. Don't cry.

She turned and walked across the road to the airport. She looked back once, to see Uncle Yazzie standing there, just as he had all those years ago, waving after her sadly. The pain, the terror she'd felt walking into the unknown washed over her again. The loss of her family.

Oh, God.

She tore her gaze away and headed into the airport. There were a few other passengers waiting for the plane to Sitka. Evelyn checked in and then found a spot in the farthest corner of the airport. She stared down at the box and the card from Léelk'w.

She opened the card first.

Evie, you're scared of opening your heart again. You've suffered so much pain and loneliness. I understand the loss, but you cannot run from your ghosts. You need to embrace them, for they make up who you are. Your life will be empty if you don't accept who you are.

These were your mother's. She made them herself and wanted you to have them when you became a woman. They're overdue coming into your possession. Wear them and remember us.

And forgive, my love. Forgive yourself. Your family.

Come back soon.

Love, Léelk'w.

Tears streamed down her face and she opened the box. There were the abalone earrings that shimmered and were smooth. Her mother's.

Like a long-forgotten memory she heard her mother's voice in her head, singing a traditional song and brushing her hair.

For so long Evelyn had locked all those memories away, making her restless. She'd forgotten who she was. She'd lost her family, herself. The pain had been unbearable, but now she had a chance to have it all back.

Love was worth the risk.

She loved Derek. She loved Mo.

She wanted to be in their life.

She deserved happiness.

She wasn't being selfish, pursuing happiness.

She wanted to stay in Wolf's Harbor—the place where she was born. It was in her blood. And she wanted to help Derek get a hospital here, so that women could safely have their children. So those who were severely injured could get treatment right away.

She wanted Wolf's Harbor to grow.

And she wanted to grow here.

She was tired of running. The way to make things right was to stay. To take her father's place and make amends with Jocelyn and Martha.

She wasn't her father, but she was their family too.

"Ladies and gentlemen, we'll now begin boarding for our non-stop flight to Sitka. Please have your boarding passes ready and line up at Gate One."

Evelyn pocketed the earrings and grabbed her bag, but instead of heading to the gate she ran outside.

Uncle Yazzie was still sitting there, gazing at the plane, and she could see tears in his eyes.

"Uncle Yazzie!" Evelyn shouted.

Joe Sr. turned around and grinned. "I thought my mother was crazy when she said you'd change your mind. You have a stubborn streak like your mother did and *she* never changed her mind."

Evelyn laughed and they hugged each other.

"Welcome home, Evie."

"It's good to be home, Uncle Yazzie."

She wasn't sure if Derek would have her, but she had to take the chance. Either way, she was staying in Wolf's Harbor and she was going to help Derek get that hospital—and if that was all her relationship with Derek could be, then so be it.

She wasn't going anywhere.

She was home.

Derek sat next to Jocelyn.

He was numb. He felt completely numb again.

"What happened?" Jocelyn moaned.

"You fainted and you have a concussion."

"Martha?"

"Frank is with her. She's okay, and Tim has checked on the baby. Still a strong heartbeat."

"Tim? I thought that Evelyn was your OB/GYN."

"Evelyn had to go to Seattle," Derek said stonily.

"Oh." Jocelyn closed her eyes. "I said something to her, didn't I?"

"Painkillers can lower inhibitions."

Jocelyn groaned. "Has she left? I need to apologize."

"Yes. She's left."

"She was a child and confused," Jocelyn said. "Thorne was distracted and the weather didn't help. You can't blame a kid. I feel terrible. Sure, I was the villain in her story as a child, but I see she doesn't think that way anymore. She's the villain in her own story. She blames herself."

Derek saw that. He recalled the things she'd said. She did blame herself. She said she'd ruin his life. But she wasn't to blame and she was denying herself any shot at love and happiness because she was punishing herself.

"You remind me of Thorne, Dr. Taylor."

"How so?"

"Widower, lonely with a child. Afraid… But I don't think you're too scared to move forward now. Thorne didn't forget his wife. He loved her. But he told me that his heart expanded."

"What?" Derek asked.

"I know it sounds silly, and I didn't get it until he died. There I was, devastated that the man I loved had died. I was left pregnant and alone. Thorne was the love of my life and I thought I'd never get over him. But a few years went by, and I just existed day to day, being a mother to Martha, and then I met Frank. I realized then what Thorne meant. A heart is not restricted to one person—it expands to encompass many people in your life. I will always love Thorne, but my heart has room for Frank too."

A tear slid down Derek's cheek and he wiped it away as Jocelyn's words sank in. He couldn't go on living this half-life. He was still alive and he had to *live*.

Even though he'd tried not to let it happen his heart had expanded and Evelyn had wormed her way in. He loved the way she was with his daughter. She said she didn't want kids, but he understood her fear. Evelyn had lost so much in her life—it was why she ran.

They were the same.

He loved her and he couldn't lose her. He'd convince her to stay. If she wouldn't he'd leave Wolf's Harbor—he would. He would follow her anywhere. He had to grieve. He had to forgive himself. He had to heal and move on.

He had to stop Evelyn from getting on that plane before it was too late.

"I've got to go, Jocelyn. Thanks."

Jocelyn nodded and smiled. "Tell her I'm sorry."

Derek nodded and left the exam room. He grabbed his jacket and checked his watch. He was hoping he would make it before the Sitka flight left.

He ran out of the clinic and stopped dead in his tracks when he saw Joe Yazzie's cab pull up on the other side of the street.

Evelyn got out and stood there. She crossed the street. His heart skipped a beat.

She stayed.

"What're you doing here?" Derek asked, stunned. "I thought you were going to Sitka."

"I was, but…" She was trembling. "I lost my family once and I blamed myself for that loss."

"You punished yourself," he said gently.

Tears welled in her eyes. "Yes."

"You don't need to punish yourself. It wasn't your fault. Jocelyn explained."

"She did?" Evelyn asked quizzically.

"You were a *child*, Evelyn. You didn't kill your father. A truck did."

She nodded. "I hardened my heart to love. I was so afraid of being hurt, of hurting someone or being left alone again. Having no feelings was easier. I thought so, but it's not. I love you. I love Mo. I thought I didn't deserve you both because I ruined so many lives. But I didn't ruin them. I was ruining just one—my own. I don't want to be bitter or emotionless anymore. I want to *feel* again."

Derek cut off her babbling by closing the gap between them and cupping her face, kissing her. Her arms, shaking, came around him and she melted into him.

"I love you too, Evelyn."

She beamed up at him. "You do?"

"For so long I thought I couldn't love again. I thought you only got one love. But my heart has expanded and you're firmly in there. I can't lose you, Evelyn. Even if it means I have to leave here and go where you need to go, I will. You brought me back to life."

Tears slid down her cheeks. "You brought me back to life too."

They kissed again.

"So... Seattle?"

"What?" she asked.

"You said you were going there."

Evelyn grinned and then kissed him. "We're not going anywhere. I just came home and I want to stay here—if you think the clinic can use me."

Derek picked her up and spun her around, set her back down. "I love you, Evelyn Saunders, and I never thought I would feel this way again. You've brightened my life. You breathed life into me and Mo again. I was just existing. I wasn't alive. I was numb to it all. But you've given me purpose. I love you."

He kissed her again and wrapped his arms tightly around her, holding her tight.

He was finally awake.

He was alive again.

And although he would never forget Vivian, he felt as if he could feel, breathe and live again. For the first time in a long, long time.

He was whole once more.

EPILOGUE

One year later

EVELYN STOOD IN front of the construction site, staring up at the hospital that was being erected in Wolf's Harbor. Since she'd taken on the position as permanent OB/GYN there, Juneau General Hospital and the state of Alaska had invested funds to make Wolf's Harbor Community Health Center a reality.

Evelyn had to go to Juneau and teach classes a few times a year, but that was no problem for her. Or at least it hadn't been until last month.

She touched her round belly. Soon she'd have to stop traveling to Juneau and back, but there was another OB/GYN who'd come to work permanently at the clinic and would be taking over Evelyn's position while she was on maternity leave.

Tim Vance had also signed up to stay on permanently as another general practitioner, which meant Derek wasn't tied down so much.

More staff were being hired, and the small hospital was on schedule to open by the end of the month.

"What're you staring at?" Derek asked, coming to stand beside her.

"The sign is crooked."

Derek squinted up at the sign. "It is not. It's fine."

"Hmm…" She rubbed her belly as the baby kicked. "It's almost time to pick up Mo from school, isn't it?"

"Yep—you want to walk down together? I'm done for the day and I'm letting Janet handle the nurse interviews over Skype. She'll pick good ones."

Evelyn nodded and took Derek's hand as they walked down Main Street toward the school. "Martha is taking online courses to get her nursing degree."

"That's great. But I don't know how she's managing that and taking care of her little girl. Ever since her little one started walking she's been rambunctious. Do you know how many stitches I've had to put in that kid's head?"

Evelyn laughed. "Jocelyn said she keeps her on her toes. It'll be nice to have more young families here. This hospital is breathing new life into Wolf's Harbor."

Derek nodded. "I just hope no one makes fun of Joe the Third."

Evelyn laughed. "Why would they?"

"Joe *the Third*?"

Evelyn chuckled again. "Yeah, well, it's a tradition."

"I don't think Katlian was too pleased with having to hand you over to me, though."

"Léelk'w likes you—and she loves Mo."

"Mo loves her."

"Léelk'w's heart has always had room for all her family."

Derek kissed her hand. "I'm just glad she's not giving me too much of a hard time anymore."

They stopped at the school yard just as the bell rang and Mo came running out of the small community school, her purple backpack a dead giveaway as she ran toward them.

"Dad! Evie!"

Mo ran past Derek and went to greet the baby first, before kissing her father and then Evelyn.

"Did you have a good day?"

"Yep! And I ate all my lunch. Can we go to Sally's?"

"I think so," Derek said.

"Yes! Ice cream!" Mo said, pumping her fist.

"Not ice cream. Not before dinner," Derek said.

"I could do with some ice cream," Evelyn teased.

Derek rolled his eyes. "Fine. Ice cream."

"Yes! Ice cream!" Mo shouted again, fist-pumping harder.

"Who taught you to fist-pump?" Evelyn asked as they walked away from the school toward Sally's.

"Léelk'w," Mo said.

"Of course she did," Derek said dryly.

Mo skipped ahead and Derek followed close behind her, while Evelyn walked slowly, her heart swelling as she watched her little family run ahead. The baby in her belly kicked and she smiled, rubbed where the baby had kicked.

She wasn't sure what Mo was going to think about having a baby brother...

She was definitely not calling him Joe the Fourth.

Thorne was good option.

She smiled as Derek picked up Mo and swung her around.

Maybe Derek Jr.?

There was time still to name the baby.

She picked up her pace to catch up with her family.

She was glad that she had finally found her place.

She was glad that she was finally home.

* * * * *

LET'S TALK

Romance

For exclusive extracts, competitions
and special offers, find us online:

f facebook.com/millsandboon

⊙ @millsandboonuk

🐦 @millsandboon

Or get in touch on 0844 844 1351*

For all the latest titles coming soon,
visit millsandboon.co.uk/nextmonth

*Calls cost 7p per minute plus your phone company's price per
minute access charge